T0195776

"I am Arrah, and I am from the Realm of Myr."

Traeth did not doubt her words. "You are a swan maiden," he affirmed.

"Aye." Her body tensed and her gaze covertly slipped back to her swan skin at his feet. She reached for it.

He stopped her hand. He stooped and captured her feather skin in his own tight grasp.

In a widening flash her eyes penetrated him more surely than cold steel. "That is mine. I cannot return to Myr without it."

"I claim your swan feathers and your woman's body as my own," he said boldly.

And then he saw the shift of her eyes from a cajoling magenta blue to red, hot fire. "You, foolish man, are lower than the lowest crawler in the bog to take that freedom which is mine. I did not choose you!"

"No matter." His voice was wholly arrogant. "I have chosen you."

"Then you have chosen trouble, foolish man. . . ."

Books by Betina Lindsey

Waltz with the Lady
Swan Bride
The Serpent Beguiled
Swan Witch
Swan Star

Published by POCKET BOOKS

SWAN STAR

Betina Lindsey

POCKET BOOKS

New York   London   Toronto   Sydney   Tokyo   Singapore

This book is a work of fiction. Names, characters, places and incidents are products of the author's imagination or are used fictitiously. Any resemblance to actual events or locales or persons, living or dead, is entirely coincidental.

An *Original* Publication of POCKET BOOKS

POCKET BOOKS, a division of Simon & Schuster Inc.
1230 Avenue of the Americas, New York, NY 10020

ISBN: 978-1-5011-3375-6

First Pocket Books printing August 1994

10 9 8 7 6 5 4 3 2 1

POCKET and colophon are registered trademarks of Simon & Schuster Inc.

Cover art by Aleta Jenks

Printed in the U.S.A.

To my daughter Eowyn,
who's a pixie,
a fairy sprite and
a Renaissance maiden all in one

Love is like a star,
unchangeable in an eternal heaven.
Love is here,
Love is now.

SWAN STAR

Chapter

1

Star by star over the Loch of the Dragon's Mouth arose the evening. Elusive as dreams, yet vivid as a promise given, even in midsummer, the loch was as solemn and chilly as a banshee's breath. Across the face of the moon, appearing shadowy and huge, winged a pair of white swans. Spiraling down, both alighted and glided to shore. Wild-winged shape-shifters, a young woman and a girl shed their swan skins in a chimera of down, feathers and phantasm.

A wigeon flew a little way, uttering a soft call. Arrah of Myr listened. Her watchful eyes scanned the forested hills and the rocky cliffs that shelved like giant stairways.

"It seems safe enough," she said to her young companion. She left her swan skin ashore and stepped back into the water.

The silence cloaked her naked body as she floated in the loch. Night deepened and mystery crept around her from every side. Upon this midsummer's eve, she felt her share of nervousness for succumbing to Sib's pleas and her own need for just a wee bit of adventure.

On a whim, she and her young swan sister, Sib, had left the realm of Myr and crossed over on a ley path into the world of men to have a "look-see," as Sib put it. Myr, the ancient haven of the swan maidens, was an enchanted place and very much different from the world of men. All her life Arrah had heard tales of men, but she'd never seen one . . . and a part of her wondered if she truly wanted to. Tradition held that the first kiss between a man and swan maiden would leave the man hopelessly enchanted.

"Which star did I come from?" asked Sib, now floating beside her.

Arrah did not look over at her, but kept her eyes skyward. Sib always needed the assurance that she was star-born. Oh, Arrah could not blame her. Sib was impatient to transform from child to woman.

Arrah remembered her own anxiety and gawkiness before chrysalis, the time when a swan maiden changes into a woman. She thought of the time she'd lived alone in the forest sulking and hiding from her own wretched reflection. She'd wanted to be beautiful, like the other swan maidens of Myr. She'd tried to sing, but nothing but a dull croak had ever passed her lips. Her skin had been rough and scaly and her eyes a dull gray. Her hair—she'd despaired that it would ever be more than a briery thatch sticking out from her head. When at last she'd accepted herself as she was, almost magically she'd begun to slowly transform. She knew now that one must find out for oneself that beauty's perfection pays no heed to the surface, but comes from what lies beneath.

"Listen," she advised Sib. "Lose yourself in the silence. The silence stretches and connects to the stars and to the one star that your soul comes from. You will find your star in the silence among all stars."

Sib remained quiet.

Arrah searched and found her own star amidst the myriad of sparkling diadems. She knew that each soul coming from a different star brought a different quality of love's essence. Some brought love that was strong, others a love that was compassionate. Some brought love that was wise, expansive as a cloudless sky. Some brought love that was childlike, gentle, like the sweet fragrance of roses, while some brought love's fire, scorching as sunset. Each time someone risked to feel the love of another, the light of their two stars joined.

Suddenly, the blare of a horn broke the stillness. Sib splashed upright. "Where did that come from?"

Her own heart quickening, Arrah said, "'Tis from the castle, on the far shore of the loch. Look, and you can see the torches lighting the battlements."

"Truly?" marveled Sib, squinting her elfin eyes. "Maybe we should go closer and see this castle."

"We'll go no closer than this. 'Tis not safe for us. 'Tis the abode of the Fianna."

"And who be the Fianna?"

Arrah was not sure herself, but repeated what she had learned from others who had crossed over in times before. "Men. Men who are ruthless warriors pledged to an even more ruthless chieftain."

"Beway," breathed Sib with astonishment.

"The Fianna are not of our kith. Though the bond of love can run deep and strong between our two races, it can end badly, for it carries a great price, including death."

"You tell me only the worst," pouted Sib. "I have heard that such a union can also bring a joy that can live for centuries beyond death."

"'Tis an idle tale for young maidens to dream upon," scoffed Arrah.

Sib turned and began to swim toward the mossy bank.

"Where are you going?" Arrah called out.

"I'm going to fly over to this castle and take a look at these Fianna."

Sib was unpredictable.

Arrah kicked up a froth of water in trying to catch up with her. She had learned the hard way, through the seasons of Sib's childhood, that she was a sorceress of small disasters.

Out of breath, Arrah climbed onto the bank after Sib. "Be warned, the Fianna take great sport in shooting down flying game with their arrows and crossbows. We should return to Myr."

"Not until I've seen the Fianna!" declared Sib stubbornly.

"Then you will see alone!" announced Arrah just as stubbornly.

Already Sib was reaching for her feather skin and melding into her swan form.

"I'll not go with you!" reaffirmed Arrah, seeing no advantage in herself being endangered along with her foolish sister. Helplessly, she watched Sib winging upwind across the loch toward the castle's three towers. She sat down on the soft, mossy growth and sighed with defeat. She would wait until Sib returned. If return she did. Oh, why could Sib not behave herself? Where was her common sense?

Arrah's emotions were churning. She'd never had such a clash of wills with Sib. In Myr their differences were easily and harmoniously settled. What had gotten into them both?

Mayhap it was the crossing from one realm to another. She wriggled her toes in the lap of gentle waves. The old tales told that before the loch this place had been the abode of a giant fire-breathing dragon that guarded the boundaries between the mortal world and that of Faerie. A power-hungry sorcerer had tricked the dragon into opening its great mouth to spew out fire, whereupon the sorcerer conjured a cloudburst that filled the dragon's mouth and doused its fire. The loch was formed, and since that time the borderlands had been left unguarded and become wild, spell-haunted places where no mortal or fairy could be safe.

Arrah sighed sadly. Even now in Myr dragons were a rarity, and in the world of men they were no more. She had little tolerance for the puffed-up gallants who thought it their knightly duty to slay dragons. Surely that was the difference between the world of men and Myr. In Myr one did not slay dragons, one embraced them.

She shifted and looked over her shoulder. Was she alone? She breathed the air, and a hundred fragrances bombarded her nostrils. Since childhood she'd assisted Terwen, the herbalist, on herb-gathering forays into the forests and meadows. With her eyes closed, by fragrance alone Arrah could ferret out both rare and common herbs.

To fill the time, she began sorting scents. Cloyingly, heliotrope wafted on the air at her left, while from forest shadows swirled the deceptively sweet but poisonous monkshood. She breathed deeply and attempted to release her nervousness.

She felt chilled and made to reach for her feather skin, but in the darkness she could not see it. Instead, she drew up her legs and rested her chin in her hands upon her knees and listened for the wingbeat of her sister's return.

Faintly, she could hear the whisper of harp drifting over the loch from the castle. Now, the curious part of her wished she had gone with Sib to spy upon the Fianna behind tall stone walls. She would like to see the fine ladies who wore more than feather cloaks and down spun gowns. She might have glimpsed a bold warrior in fiery torchlight walking the battlements. She'd not seen a man close up before . . . and decidedly not one so notorious as a Fiannan.

As she contemplated this, something akin to discontent troubled her for the first time. The peace, tranquillity and primeval forests of Myr seemed not to be enough; nor was the wild rejoicing of flight when every feather sings, nor the wonder of Myr's magical realm, nor even the dance of the swan maidens on the night of the full moon.

Arrah longed for something more . . . but she was not sure what that something was.

She could not tell when she first knew she was not alone. The eerie sensation began to tingle unpleasantly at the ends of her nerves; she felt a sudden urge to turn and flee. But she forced herself to sit quietly, lifting her eyes to the sky above. Subtly, fresh sweat and an ambery-musk scent hit her nostrils. Her chin lifted and with a slow inward breath she smelled the air. The scent was familiar, yet new. She sifted through a myriad of possibilities, and then the knowing struck her. She smelled a man. . . .

On bent knee, Traeth of Rhune crouched on the forest edge. His black eyes held hard on the lone woman sitting beside the loch. With fascination he had watched her small companion transform into a swan and fly off. Like most, he knew well the lore surrounding the race of swans. To kill one would bring death to the killer. To kiss one would bring endless ecstasy . . . but at great price.

He shifted his bow to rest upon his shoulder and contemplated the advantage in capturing her. Her feather skin lay within his reach. He had but to claim it and she would be his.

Wisely, he hesitated. Traeth was a cautious man. He'd no wish to fall victim to a swan maiden's bewitchments. In his youth he'd been warned often enough by his mentor, Carne the Aged, "to be leery of women, especially fairy women."

Yet, he watched the swan maiden. Pale and golden-haired, her elusive charm held him spellbound. But he was no fool: She would be a weaver of magicks.

He stepped out of the forest cover, seeing where this

enchantress had laid her swan feathers, and stepped to one side of her feather skin.

He spoke forthrightly. "What is your name, lady, and from where do you come?"

She jumped to her feet and turned about. Wariness marked her fair features. Her eyes darted to her swan feathers and then back to him before she spoke.

"I am Arrah, and I am from the realm of Myr."

Her voice was sweetly lilting. He did not doubt her words, for one of the swan race could not lie. "You are a swan maiden," he affirmed.

"Aye." Her body tensed and her gaze covertly slipped back to the swan skin. "You must be a man."

He smiled. "Aye, I am that."

"I've not met a man before." Her eyes held him, spilling into his a sense of childlike curiosity, a rare innocence and a sense of wonder.

He felt an awkward shyness, an embarrassment, two emotions he'd exiled long ago. After all, he was a seasoned warrior of the Fianna; he could not display emotion.

"Ahh," he breathed slowly. "So, allow me to present myself." He gave his most gallant bow. "I am Traeth of Rhune, a man."

There was a lengthy silence after that as she made a slow, deliberate appraisal of him. He supposed no one had ever told her that it was rude to stare, and he decided not to be the first, for he liked her clear-eyed gaze upon him.

"So?" he asked finally. "What do you think of this man before you?"

She shifted and clasped her hands together before her soft belly. Inwardly, he felt the strongest desire to reach out and caress that softness.

"I . . . I think you are handsome."

"Handsome? Only that?" he quizzed lightly. "And how can you say that I am handsome if you've never seen another man?"

7

She looked puzzled, then said, "I like looking at you, so you must be handsome."

He warmed to her honesty. "And milady, I like looking at you as well. Does that mean you are beautiful?"

"Aye, it does," she said without false modesty. "All swan maidens are beautiful. Did you not know this?"

"I did not, though 'tis a matter of legend. But I've not always believed in legends."

"Why not?" she asked, taking a step toward him.

"Because legends are legends and most end badly, especially legends about lovers."

"Mayhap," she said, her brow wrinkling slightly, "we are fond of hearing tragedies because we hope that weeping over other people's misadventures will spare us our own."

"Mayhap," he echoed, thinking not of love gone awry but of how long it might take to seduce her into his arms. He asked politely, "Would you like to walk and talk beside the loch?"

She giggled. The sound was a sweet chiming to his ears.

She said, "You must be a poet or a rhymer."

"Nay, I am neither." He chose not to elaborate that he was a slayer of man, beast and reptile, which ofttimes could be all in one.

She had already started walking along the loch's edge, halting occasionally to dabble her toes in the water. The moon, which was rising higher in the sky, had turned translucent silver and was casting a light that illuminated the perfect outline of her body.

He caught up with her, admiring her natural state of gracefulness. She turned and walked on and he followed. She gave him an oblique glance and then slowed by a step until she was parallel.

'Twas not a common pastime of his to walk with a woman along the loch. Oddly, he felt as if he had never seen a woman before, at least not a woman like her. She was unusually tall, although he was taller. Her eyes attracted him. They were swirling rainbows of changing colors. Her skin was white, smooth as porcelain. Her hair was a mass of voluptuous golden tangles braided haphazardly, with here and there a tucking of flowers.

As if she knew his thoughts, she questioned, "Am I different from the women of your realm?"

"Why do you ask?"

"Because you stare at me. In the realm of Myr 'tis rude to stare, but I know customs are different here."

He cleared his throat, feeling somewhat amused, but exposed. "Aye, you are different and the same."

"In what ways—ouch!" She stumbled and shifted her weight to one foot. "I've caught a thorn in my toe."

She sank down and sat on the flat surface of a boulder. He knelt beside her on one knee, took her small tapered foot in hand and examined it.

"Do you see it? The light is poor," she said, nose to nose with him. He plucked it out and then did an unexpected thing: He put his lips to her toe and sucked the tiny wound.

Arrah felt as if she'd been touched by fire. Her face flamed like sunrise and she looked at him wonderingly.

He drew back and in one glimpse saw her fluster. "I'm sorry; it stops the bleeding."

She nodded her head, understanding that, but not understanding how his touch could have quickened her senses so fully.

"Your toes," he went on. "The women in my realm don't have thin webbing between their toes. That is one way you are different."

He was still cradling her foot in his hand, and he caressed it gently as he spoke. The power of his touch was like a current surging up her leg and pooling in between her thighs. First stroking lightly and then pressing harder, he rubbed and played his thumbs and forefingers over her toes, then released them. But one finger continued to stroke, circling.

Beway! Great Goddess! Arrah nearly passed out from the pleasure. There were few places upon her body that were as sensitive as the webbing between her toes.

"Another difference is your eyes. I've not seen eyes with the shifting colors of opals," he remarked, dropping his hand away.

Arrah wanted to say, "Don't stop!" She was inwardly humming from his ministering, from his musky scent, from the smell of his leathers. She imagined what his hair would smell like if she were to nuzzle her face in it. It was thick with the matte-chestnut sheen that comes from wind and sun.

He offered her a hand up, and then as they walked he let his arm drop about her waist. She leaned into him, her hip fitting neatly against his, her shoulder resting in the concave beneath his arm.

"Our eyes do change colors with our moods," she said. "But ofttimes 'tis a disadvantage, for all can see if you are angry or jealous or sad. Nothing is hidden for long."

"I have never understood the whims of women. They cry for no reason, become closemouthed and fall into sulks."

"It seems you have a low opinion of women. Mayhap you've never been loved by one."

He scratched his chin thoughtfully. "Indeed, I've been teased and toyed with, but never loved."

"Then no woman has ever sung her love lilt to you," she said sadly.

"No woman has ever sung to me a single note. What is a love lilt?"

"'Tis an oath of trust and surrender. A swan maiden sings her love lilt to the man she wishes to mate lifelong with. After her love lilt is sung, her heart will never be given to another."

"Och, I don't think I've met the woman I would mate lifelong with."

"Have you loved a woman?"

"Once or twice." He gave a rueful smile. "Since the warrior maiden, Calleen, I have trusted no woman. Before that I trusted them all."

"Did she betray your trust?"

"Aye, she did, and seven years to this very night. She rejected me for the flatterer MacRoth. Oh, it hurt my youthful pride, but I bid good riddance to them both . . . that is, after I bested Calleen in a match of swords. Now, my heart is not easily won, nor my passion quickly aroused."

A silky thread of expectation glided beneath his words. His mind kept moving ahead. He looked over at her full-faced and grinned. She grinned back, and something clicked into place between them.

She turned about and said, "I'd like to sit on the shore."

"Whatever you wish," he yielded.

She walked slightly ahead of him, conscious of his eyes upon her. A little warmth still glowed in the confines of her womb, a small contraction, as his hand brushed across her back. He spread his black cloak upon the ground and Arrah sat down.

She had forgotten Sib. She cast a watchful glance across the loch toward the castle, then turned her attention back to Traeth of Rhune.

There was nothing about him that was not rough and coarse. The stubborn line of his chin, the high cheekbones, the dark head set proudly on the powerful width of his shoulders, even his boots that were spurred with heavy silver and that reached almost to his muscled thighs. His brows were thickly ridged in the middle, making him look very serious, until he smiled.

They both smiled, she thought, like smug, delighted children sharing a secret.

His eyes swept over her and settled on her face. "When you return to your realm of Myr you'll have a tale or two to tell now you have met a man."

"That I have. But it was not as exciting as I thought, and not much of a tale to tell."

"What?" His voice raised with mock offense. "Surely you'll have something to say about your adventure."

She touched her chin thoughtfully. "I shall say . . . each of you must venture into the world of men and see a man for yourself, for a man is beyond description."

A sudden, she heard a familiar *whilloo* in the distance. She turned sharply to the sound. Where was Sib?

"Is something amiss?" he asked.

"Nay, it's just that I should be returning soon. . . ."

The *whilloo* sounded again and this time even he turned an ear to the call.

She knew Sib was waiting for her and dared not approach. Leaning forward, Arrah reached for the swan skin, which lay very close to the hand of Traeth of Rhune.

Traeth had not intended to detain her, but oddly enough, he despaired at the thought of her leaving him. Never had he been so aroused by a woman, or so acutely aware of it. With much difficulty, he kept his attention on her face. It took a great effort not to follow the beginning curve of soft breast down to the flow of white hip. Flawless as alabaster, she was the most beautiful woman he'd ever seen.

He felt his body tighten with desire as he imagined her lying beneath him on soft furs, her lips swollen from his kisses, her slender legs opening to his passion. He did not want her to leave.

He caught her hand and put it to his lips. "Will you return again?"

"Do you wish it?" she asked.

"I wish it," he said firmly. His fingers touched a swatch of her golden hair. He turned it over and over in his hand, examining its texture and moonlit shimmer. He let loose her hair and caressed the smooth curve of her neck and throat, up to her moisture-glistened lips. His thumb lightly brushed the softness of her mouth. A tingling from the faint breeze of her warm breath flowed over his thumb tip, lingering. He remained very still, his desire burning, all common sense slipping from his mind. He wanted her.

"I will think on it. I have heard many things about this realm, and few are good." She drew away her hand and reached again for her swan skin.

He halted her arm. The deed was done so swiftly it was as if someone other than he had done it. Without taking his eyes from her, he captured and claimed her feather skin.

In a widening flash, her eyes penetrated him more surely than cold steel. "That is mine. I cannot return to Myr without it."

"I know," he said. Her vulnerability lay not in the swan skin in his grasp, but in her pure innocence . . . an innocence he himself had lost a hundred battles ago.

He hoped she would not fall down upon her knees and beg, for he'd no intention of giving in. Admirably, for all her naïveté, she held nothing of humility in her demeanor. Defiance marked her form and offense her fine face.

"Did you hear me?" she said again, her tone circumspect.

"I did," came his steadfast reply.

"Then let loose of it." Her lips tightened.

"No," he said in the unyielding tone of a seasoned warrior. "I claim your swan feathers and your woman's body as my own."

And then he saw the shift in her eyes from a cajoling magenta blue to red-hot fire. "You, Traeth of Rhune, are lower than the lowest crawler in the bog to take that freedom which is mine. I did not choose you!"

"No matter." His voice was wholly arrogant. "I have chosen you."

"You have chosen trouble, foolish man," she spat. Her voice was not so lilting now.

Traeth was not moved by her threat or insult, though deep within he knew she spoke true. He was choosing trouble.

"As long as I have your swan skin, you have no choice but to come with me." He picked up her feather skin and folded it neatly. Then he offered his hand to her and without condescension invited, "Come, Lady Arrah."

Of course, she refused to take his hand. He had expected her defiance.

She folded her arms mutinously across her chest and sat rooted upon his cloak. "Where am I to come?"

"You are to come to Rhune Castle with me. 'Tis my abode."

"I do not like castles," she said haughtily.

"Mayhap, you'll like this one."

"Mayhap, I won't."

Anger surged through Arrah's blood, warming it to life again. She was well aware of the figure she made, huddled on his cloak like nothing so much as a waif. He stood above her, seeming as tall as the dark hills behind him, his boots wide apart and his thumbs in the wide leather belt at his waist.

"I'll not ask twice," he said.

"I'll not come once," she said.

He turned about and, with the feather skin tucked tightly under his arm, began walking.

Never before had she felt such ire as she did sitting upon his cloak beside the black loch. Never before had she met and been attracted to so callous a person as he. Nor had she ever imagined the world in which she so unexpectedly found herself, where a person might take another's freedom at his whim.

Begrudgingly, she came to her feet, stepped off the cloak, snapped it in the air and wrapped it around her shoulders. Sullenly, she followed a few paces behind him. By his long stride she saw he felt confident she would follow. She had no choice—he possessed her swan skin.

Chapter

Arrah struggled against the panic rising slowly in her throat and the sense of foreboding as she looked upon the high towers of Rhune Castle. It towered, a great mass of grim stone, above the Loch of the Dragon's Mouth. Marveling, she saw the battlements etched high against the night sky, and the tall towers that reflected the moonlight in their embrasures while the sheer wall beneath lay in cold shadows. There was nothing about the castle that was not stark and forbidding. Carved from somber stone, it had a bleak air as inhospitable and threatening as the wild mountains surrounding it.

As she surveyed her first castle, her mouth hung open and her eyes widened, for in silhouette it appeared to be a magnificent gray dragon rearing up over the loch. She pressed her chilled hands against the warmth of her body beneath the cloak and reminded herself to be strong. She watched the iron portcullis lift slowly above the carved arching dragon gate. Back straight, though her heart was still coursing with apprehension, she walked at the heels of Traeth over the drawbridge and beneath the iron-fanged port-cullis.

"This pile of stones is my home," said Traeth over his shoulder. "Please follow me into my dwelling, milady."

She begrudged him the long, effortless stride that marked him as one who was adept at scaling rocky crags and breaking through forest thickets. He had covered the distance with a careless swiftness that won her respect and her irritation. She would have preferred to fly, but then he was clutching her swan skin in his warrior's hand. She'd vowed not to let him or her swan skin from her sight. At the first moment she would steal it back and fly.

He spoke to someone peering from a barbican above her head, his cool voice warming slightly with laughter. "Aye, 'tis fowl I bring to our table this festive night."

Arrah found no humor in such a remark.

Rhune Castle was astir. The guardrooms on either side of the passageway through the keep were bustling with his clansmen at evening meal.

In the yard, lit with flaring torches, great hounds snarled over bones and long-maned destriers snorted and pawed the earth restlessly. She saw more Fianna, tall men with broad shoulders, elven chain mail covering their chests and swords at their sides. She felt their unrelenting gaze rake over her.

"Keep your eyes to yourself, lad," he said curtly to one, and the youth dropped his eyes hastily. "Take heart," he said, putting a protective arm about her shoulders. "They'll not eat you alive . . . at least not yet."

His jest was little comfort. Boldly, with her chin up and her head high, she stepped past them, determined that none should guess at the fearful anticipation touching her.

He took her through a tower door and up circular

stairs. She'd never seen the like or been within so confined a space. It looked like a cave, and felt as darkly mysterious. His hand beneath her arm steadied her as they continued on an interminable distance. Finally, he paused before a tall door, heavily carved and studded with brass.

"This is your chamber," he said, and kicked the door open with a thrust of his boot. He stood aside, waiting for her to enter.

She drew a deep breath, not knowing what to expect, for she'd dwelled the whole of her life in a clement forest beside a magical lake. How did one live in a castle?

"Go along, milady," he urged, looking as if he might give her a small push.

The chamber was in near darkness. She walked only a few steps, then paused until her eyes grew accustomed to the dim light. Candles guttered fitfully in dragon sconces above an enormous fireplace. The fire had died to a bed of coals and black shadows stretched from the high ceiling to the far corners of the room to meet across the stone floor. Her eyes riveted to more dragons rearing up beside the hearth. She looked to the casement window that yawned open and a shiver trembled through her, for across the mouth were iron bars.

I am a prisoner of Rhune Castle, she thought. Then she said aloud, "'Tis not a friendly place."

"Aye," he smiled ruefully, as if he also knew that was so.

He left her and crossed the room to a heavy chest. She watched intently as he opened it. He rummaged through the contents, took some garments out and carefully lay her swan skin inside. He closed the lid and took something small from a ring at his waist. Then she heard a click.

"What is it you are doing with my swan skin?" she asked.

"I am locking it in this chest for safekeeping."

"Safekeeping? Locking? . . ." She did not understand this.

"Aye," he said, holding up a small metal object.

"What is that in your hand?"

"A key, milady. 'Tis the key to the chest. I have locked your cloak inside the chest," he explained.

"If I do not have that key I cannot get it back," she said.

He nodded. "That is the idea."

"That is not right. I have never seen such a thing."

"You don't have locks and keys in Myr?"

"No. Why should we?"

"To protect those things you value from thieves."

"There are no thieves in Myr. What belongs to one belongs to all. Besides, the feather skin is mine. 'Tis you who is the thief here and 'tis you who has the lock and key. That makes no sense to me."

Amusement flickered in his eyes. "Aye, you do have a point." He shrugged. "Mayhap I am a thief, though none but you has dared to accuse me of such a deed before."

"How do you bear the shame of it?"

"Like I bear all else, dear lady—like a man in the world of men."

"And how is that?"

"You ask too many questions."

"I do not think there is such a thing as too many questions."

"Be sure that in this moment there might be," he said intolerantly.

She wanted to say more, but with great effort she held her tongue. Her eyes did not leave the key, which he hooked to others on a leather thong at his waist.

Coming toward her and holding out the garments, he said, "You must wear clothing. We've no women or womanly things at Rhune Castle, so you will wear these leggings and tunic for now."

She took a step back. He must have noticed, for he said, "I will not harm you. You can speak and move freely."

Skeptically, she directed her gaze to the iron bars and then back to him. "You've just forbid me to ask questions. How can I speak and move freely under this admonition?"

"Do not act the martyr. I did not say you could not ask questions, I only advised it in the moment. Go on—ask your questions, if it pleases you."

"When will you return my swan skin?" she said forthrightly.

"When I choose to," he said with cool dispassion.

"Mayhap you will choose to very soon." Her voice held warning; she was not without her own devices of retribution.

He smiled at that, catching her unawares, and she felt discounted. His dark eyes were warm as fire is warm, and they were brought to life by the small flames flickering in their depths and the humor touching his mouth.

"Nay, not soon. I'll not tease you by allowing you to think it." His face became grave, but the warmth of his smile lingered. "Again I say you've nothing to fear from me or the Fianna. Myself or one of my men will always attend you. Now dress yourself." He turned toward the door.

She wondered if he hoped to lull her into compliance; she figured he must be well aware that she, who came from the faerie realm, would not thrive in the harsh company of warriors.

"You are not so nice as you were beside the loch," she called after him. "What changed you?"

He paused at the threshold, his shoulders filling the doorway, and turned back.

"You will learn, milady, that in one man are many men," he said, and bowed. When he straightened all warmth had left his face.

"So you are more than Traeth of Rhune?"

"Aye, I am Mage of the Dragon's Mouth," he revealed, pride touching his voice. He left, and the door closed firmly behind him.

A mage. Alone, she brooded over his revelation.

She could not doubt it. She had heard of such sorcerers who shapeshifted and conjured the unspeakable. Though he was Fianna, she sensed in him something more ancient. He came from the lineage of the old gods who dwelled in tree and loch. It was in his stride, the nobleness of bearing, despite his shaggy chestnut locks. With a single word, such men might call forth a furious gale, sweeping havoc across lake and sea. In battle his voice would thunder from the very heavens, and the sound of his commands would echo wildly down the deep chasms and corries of the mountains.

Just the knowing frightened her. To be snared by a man was one thing, but to be entrapped by a mage was another. She was suddenly overwhelmed with a sinking feeling of despair. Dropping the garments, she slowly walked to the casement window and clasped the cold iron bars in her hands. The air of the chamber held the odor of confinement and stagnancy. She looked back to the chest and tears clouded her eyes.

She thought of Sib flying free and hoped she would be wise enough to return to Myr on her own.

Arrah had never felt so defeated. She eased down on her haunches, huddling in the strange room, and tried to cover herself completely with the black cloak. Though a fire smoldered in the hearth, the chamber held no warmth for her, and she wondered if she would eventually turn to stone like the hearth dragons.

A tap at the door startled her. Gathering herself, she snatched up the leggings and tunic and hastily put them on.

"Who is there?" she asked in a voice of false bravado.

"I am Carne the Aged," came the answer. "Are you hungry?"

"Aye," she said shortly, for she had not eaten since the morning.

She opened the door to him.

He was tall and gaunt with a face as bleak as the granite stones of Rhune Castle. Beway, she thought, not another sorcerer. The candlelight was behind him, shining in her face, and she hoped it was only a trick of the light that gave him such an appearance of dark mystery.

"So, you are the swan maiden," he said kindly. "My greetings, and my welcome to Rhune Castle."

He bowed, the great flowing sleeves of his saffron robe waving like ship's sails in the air. Beneath a long white beard, shiny gold chains peeked from around his neck. He was dark-visaged, with white brows that met in a scowling line across his face.

She stared, even though 'twas rude, and said, "Your kindness overwhelms me, though 'tis not by choice that I am here."

"I'm aware of that, my lady swan," he said, his voice filled with benign understanding. She liked him.

He stepped aside.

Behind him came three young pages in a silent procession. They carried trays filled with stuffed quail, honeyed meats, sweet wine, spiced fish livers and whole tiny pigs' heads. After placing the trays on a sideboard, the three left.

The sight made Arrah's queasy stomach a churning inferno. By the goddess! She could eat none of it, and without reserve turned the tray of beady-eyed pigs' heads to face the wall.

"Joints and bones!" chuckled Carne the Aged. "I knew you'd never eat them."

She turned to him quizzically. "And how did you know?"

"Because I could not eat them myself," he replied, looking about, his eyes settling upon a carved wooden chair.

"Aye," returned Arrah, her guard down. She sniffed the air. "'Tis true. A man who does not eat flesh smells different from one who eats flesh."

"And what else does your nose tell you, my lady swan?"

"You've a red pear in your pocket."

He laughed, then fetched it out and gave it to her. She licked her lower lip and bit into the juicy flesh.

Chewing and speaking with her mouth full, she said, "You also carry on your person vervain. Do not think you can slip it into my drink without me knowing."

"Hah! You are a canny one. 'Tis for my own use. I am beset with restlessness these summer nights."

"How so?"

"Dreams. Dark, foreboding dreams. I have no wish to see what I see."

"So you take the herb to stop your dreaming."

"Aye. But I am prophetic and many rely upon my dreams to foretell good and ill. So I cannot cease my dreaming altogether. 'Tis bad for my livelihood."

"So you have the 'sight.'"

"And more." He winked at her mischievously.

Her spirits lifting, she asked, "Will we be friends, you and I?"

"Oh, indeed," he assured her. "A fortnight past I dreamed your coming."

"You did . . ." Surprise marked her voice.

"I did." He seated himself in a chair beside the hearth and rested his hands on the dragon-head arms.

The dragons appeared everywhere in the chamber —snarling, smirking, grinning and grimacing on door latches, chair backs, hearthside and even woven into the scarlet tapestry drapes which hung on the great four-poster bed. Arrah wanted to ask Carne the Aged about this and many other puzzling mysteries surrounding the Fianna and this castle, and most certainly about the Mage of the Dragon's Mouth.

But right now she would settle for first things first, and so she asked, "And what did you dream?"

Having devoured the pear down to the thread of its stem, she pulled up a tuft-topped stool and sat at his feet.

"At the time my dream was a riddle." He clasped his hands together in front of his chest mindfully.

He paused. When at last his lips opened to speak, Arrah nearly fell off the stool with anticipation.

"I saw a wondrous creature, a radiant air vessel, a traveling spirit. Silent was its garment when it tread the earth or inhabited dwellings or stirred the waters. The wind raised it above the abodes of men, and the power of clouds then carried it far and wide and even higher, to light deep heaven."

"So . . . how does that pertain to me?"

"My child, 'twas you, a swan maiden, I saw."

"What else?" she asked curiously.

"What else?" His tone held offense. "That is enough." Arrah drew back, not much impressed. Of course, she reminded herself, she had to realize she was in the realm of men, where dreams had not the clarity of message they did in Myr.

Making amends, she said, "Truly, you have the sight. I'd only hoped you might have seen more—"

"More!" he broke in with impatience. "More!" he slapped his thigh. "'Tis always more. Everyone wants more. Beway"—he pointed a long bony finger at her nose—"you must live your own life as it comes. I'll not foretell it all. What purpose does that serve? If I told all, where is the adventure in it? No one can know the end at the beginning."

Not intimidated, Arrah returned, "But in the knowing one can be saved from folly."

He began to laugh. "Beway, a man's folly is the very gift of life. Folly is life's reward. And be sure, if I were to save you from one folly you'd find another to take its place."

"You are a skeptic."

"I have lived too long and seen too much. My child, you seem innocence itself. Where is it you come from?"

"The realm of Myr."

"Ah, Myr . . . I should have known it." His eyes widened. "The ancient heart of Earth herself. 'Twill not be easy for you here, and the Mage of the Dragon's Mouth will not readily release you."

Arrah's eyes riveted to the great chest. "My feather skin is sealed within that chest; the mage has the key. Could you not help me regain it?"

He nodded and winked at her. "Nay, for I did not help you lose it."

She dropped her chin into her hands, awash with self-recrimination. Aye, it was her own fault. She'd been careless in leaving her feather skin unattended.

She felt Carne the Aged's consoling touch on her shoulder. "I will speak to the mage on your behalf. He will listen, but in the end he always does as he chooses. He bows to no man. He was conceived from old magic."

Arrah looked up. "Och . . . I sensed it. Tell me of his origins."

"I know little enough to tell. His mother was a Tuatha woman who, in the guise of a white doe, appeared one day when his father, Bran, was hunting. She followed him to his fortress, where I served as counselor. When she was within the safety of its walls, she showed herself in her true shape—that of a beautiful woman. Bran loved her at once and kept her by him. In time she got with child, and then just before its birth, a sudden she disappeared."

"Did she return to her people?"

"No, she came here to the loch where she gave birth to Traeth. After many years of searching, Bran, who was still under the faerie woman's enchantment, died of grief and longing. 'Twas the love madness he had. In the end I found the child, Traeth. He was a wild boy who had grown up beside the loch in the deserted fortress of this castle. From the beginning, I saw he had special vision and special powers. Though he was human and trod the earth like other children, in his veins flowed magic. He was destined to live in the spell-haunted borderlands of the two realms."

"When you found him was he alone?"

"Aye, and naked with the heart of wildness itself. I cared for him a time, and then when he became more man than youth we traveled to the far country of the Morrigan. The Morrigan are women warriors, experienced, hardy, fierce and peerless in educating and teaching feats of arms. He learned all his lessons well and became a hero of the Fianna."

"Humph!" she sighed doubtfully. "I do not see much valor in him, a hero who must hold hostage one such as myself."

"There is no knowing all the tricks of a man . . . or woman's mind." He gave her a narrowed gaze. "Except for the time spent with the Morrigan, he has held himself apart from women."

"Does he not like women?"

"During our stay with the Morrigan he had a few minor flirtations, but nothing lasting. The Morrigan are independent women, not much liking home or hearth."

"I see no error in that," replied Arrah. She knew that things were different for women in the world of men—why else had so many of her swan sisters returned to Myr after their sojourns here? Aye, she realized now that men thought of women as their chattel, something to possess. Mayhap that was why Traeth's mother fled his father.

Carne the Aged smiled. "You have such a nature yourself."

"In truth I cherish my freedom—who does not?"

"But you are a woman. Unlike in your land of Myr, here in the wilds of the borderlands, a woman needs a protector."

"And who is to protect her from her protector?"

He chuckled. "I think 'tis more like who will protect her protector from her!"

Arrah frowned. "Do not expect me to join in your mirth. It is clear to me that the reason there are no women at Rhune Castle is that none are so daft as to enter."

"Mayhap," he deigned. "In my memory, you are the first to come."

"Not by my free choice, mind you."

"But you are here, nonetheless. Do not forget I saw your coming."

"And," Arrah said emphatically, "you will see my going."

"'Tis female," announced Camlan the Unsmiling, posturing before all, as was his custom.

Traeth walked a few paces around the shivering little urchin who crouched and clung to the gold-threaded hem of Camlan's blue cloak. He paused with a head shake. "How could you decipher it? I've never seen such a waif . . . she's wood rat ugly."

"I found her balancing on the parapet of the tower of the dragon's fang. She'd not a stitch on her bones," said Camlan.

Traeth bent down and peered at her. She covered her face with the cloak.

"Let loose!" commanded Camlan, pulling his cloak away. "She's not released me since I found her."

Glaring down his high, arrogant nose, he said, "I'll not be her nanny."

Traeth watched as she crouched into a fetal ball at Camlan's feet. "This midsummer's night has brought the wild things out of their boroughs, to be sure."

"It could be an omen," joined in Fergus Dry Lips from his seat before the supper table.

"An omen of ill," said Traeth flatly.

"What shall I do with her?" asked Camlan.

"You found her, so do whatever you wish. She's yours, if you can keep her from running off," Traeth said.

"I don't want her," declared Camlan.

"You not want a woman?" exclaimed Traeth. "May the gods drown me where I stand!" He'd been a companion with Camlan many years, and no man in the five kingdoms drew the eyes and hearts of woman like Camlan the Unsmiling. It was said he had a love spot on the center of his forehead, and that no woman who looked upon him could resist him, unsmiling as he was.

"I don't want this one," he said emphatically.

"Does she speak or understand us?" asked Fergus Dry Lips, ripping in two a rack of roasted lamb with his hands.

Traeth looked down and repeated the question directly to her. "Do you understand us?"

No words came from her lips, but she nodded her head affirmatively.

"Good," said Traeth in a kindly voice. "No one wants you here. So you can leave. Go back to wherever. Be off!" He made the motion of two fingers walking.

She did not move, but instead looked up beseechingly to Camlan. He sniffed, turned his back and strode over to the fire. She leaped up and followed.

"It appears you've won her affections, Camlan," smirked Fergus Dry Lips, still eating.

Traeth studied her a moment longer and then went to sit down beside Fergus at the feast table. He scratched his chin thoughtfully, aware that the urchin's appearance was not an accident. He believed that in the workings of the universe nothing was an accident. On this night of midsummer, two females entering within the walls of Rhune Castle was a portent . . . for ill or good, he could not be sure.

Beside him Fergus Dry Lips supped away. He did not necessarily chew, but broke, crunched and gulped his food. Oddly, Traeth had never noticed his uncouthness before, but now he did and it irritated him. He noticed more: the hounds scratching their flea-bitten skins by the fire, the dankness of the hall, the sour smell of his companions . . . and of himself.

When Carne the Aged entered the hall, Traeth was in a low mood. He gave no greeting as the man seated himself across the table. Unspeaking, Carne reached for bread and cheese and between sips of ale took his repast.

"So?" said Carne, finally breaking the silence between them.

"So what?" returned Traeth with false disinterest.

"I have visited the lady swan."

"Did she speak to you?"

"Aye, she did," said Carne, still chewing.

Traeth waited, but Carne did not elaborate. The old man was teasing him, he knew, but he was in no mood for it. "Aye, then?" he prodded, not hiding his interest now.

Carne put aside his cup and met Traeth's eyes with a penetrating stare. "I'll tell you out that it may cost you dearly to keep this woman. 'Tis always a mistake to trifle with a faerie woman. It cost your father his life. 'Tis a sad tale, one I've told you before and of which now I remind you again. Because of the 'love madness,' your father drove away the very woman he loved. She could not abide his jealous outbursts or his possessive tyranny. She'd no choice but to escape from him."

Traeth clenched his jaw. Were Carne any other man he might have lifted his fist to him. "True, she did escape my father, but to her own greater sorrow. She fell victim to the magicks of another sorcerer and changed into a white doe that wanders that place of the in-between. She'd have been better off to remain with my father."

"He had the love madness, she could not," Carne said harshly. "Like your mother gave your father, the swan maiden will give love for love, but she is a wild creature and out of her element. Like your mother, she will always pine for her freedom. I say release her now, before the magicks begin."

"'Tis too late," muttered Traeth.

"What do you mean?"

Traeth nodded toward the fire and Camlan the Unsmiling. The urchin still sat crouched at his feet, the firelight dancing over her ugly features. "There is another denizen of Faerie come our way this night. She's not so comely and has set her heart upon Camlan."

Carne looked at her and then turned back. Traeth saw a hint of amusement dancing about his wrinkled eyes. "And you . . . where is your heart?"

Traeth frowned, "Where it's always been—secure in the cage of bones within my chest. My sage, if you are worried, I'll assure you that I've not succumbed to any enchantments. The swan maiden holds no power over me, unless I give it."

"And will you?" Carne asked with innate persistence.

Traeth drew back with offense. "You know me better than to ask. I'm Mage of the Dragon's Mouth, master of magicks."

A slow smile crept over Carne's mouth, and then he chuckled.

"Why do you laugh?" Traeth demanded.

"Aye, I'm only agreeing," he declared, still grinning.

"Nay, I know you well enough to see you've a private mirth and I'm the brunt. Speak!"

"Nay, it cannot be told." And with that the old mystic took his leave . . . and Traeth's mood turned even darker.

Chapter

3

Time seemed suspended in this longest night of mid-summer. Though Arrah lay on the great bed of her chamber, she could not sleep. In Myr her bed was soft moss beneath a starry sky. Rhune Castle was all too strange for her. With dismay she wondered how anyone could fall asleep in a castle.

She climbed off the bed and walked over to the door. Admiringly, she touched the blackthorn surface, and in the grain she saw the wispy image of the tree spirit. It frowned. Whoever crafted this door had not bothered to ask consent from the tree spirit to chop it down. She sighed, not understanding the separation from earth spirit in this realm of men. In Myr everything was blessed and received with reverence.

She fiddled with the metal latching and after a moment opened the door. As it swung open, she saw that the lock was two-way, serving not only to keep people out but also to keep them in. Since she saw no key, she assumed that she would have no choice. The mage could lock her in as he had locked away her feather skin. The realization did not sit well with her.

Even so, she thought, *he has no need to lock me in because he is wholly confident that I will not leave . . . at least not without my feather skin.*

Endeavoring to make the best of a bad situation, she decided to find a place in the open air to sleep . . . high on the wall walk. She peeked side to side and down the corridor. The flickering light of the dragon wall sconces illuminated one way, while the other yawned like a dark mouth. Her bare feet padding along the cold stone flooring, she first chose the well-lit path. Then, pausing before an archway at the top of the stairs, she saw that the passage led down to a great hall.

She heard voices filtering up.

She had no desire to encounter the Fianna. Turning abruptly around, she took a beeswax candle from a wall sconce and set off down the shadowy corridor.

At the first cross-path, she passed beneath an arch-way of twining dragons and followed an upward, narrow, winding stairway cut inside the walls of a tower. It was a queer feeling to look about and see the unseen. Though stone, the dragons seemed to watch her from gleaming eyes.

She climbed until her calves ached and she thought of turning back, but the hope of finding her way to the wall walk and open air kept her going. A cold draft soughed past and the candle in her hand flickered weakly. A chill of uneasiness crept down her spine.

As a child in Myr she'd been told tales of the wanderers of the dark that dwelled in the borderlands. Aye, not all dark wanderers remained outside. Many, restless and grasping, took up residence between cracks of stones, in dusky corners and in eaves. Then, when darkness came, they began to stir. She could still hear Terwen's slow, whispering voice saying, "Silent as shadows, they steal among their human prey, now touching with bony fingers, now breathing pestilence, now chanting spells that bring foul dreams."

Just thinking about it, she was scaring herself. Her steps hastened. Did she hear something behind her? *Nay,* she thought, *'tis only my own footsteps.*

Then, to her great relief, the circle of her candlelight encompassed the level of a landing and a wooden door. She paused for breath and reached for the door latch. It was locked.

"Let me open it for you. You've climbed all this way."

Her heart leaping, she spun around to face the Mage of the Dragon's Mouth, standing scarcely more than a few inches from her.

"By the goddess! You booka! A weaker soul might faint away."

"I'm sorry to have frightened you, but 'tis yourself who is the snoop."

He stood insolently, thumbs in the wide leather belt at his waist. He regarded her with so much amusement in the depths of his dark eyes that her shock gave way to an embarrassment that set her cheeks aflame.

"I'm not frightened," she said with what dignity she could summon.

"Oh?" he said, one dark brow lifted with disbelief.

She felt like a child caught in an untruth, and it irritated her. She was not a child, but a woman and would be treated as such. So, in an attempt to rectify the situation, she said more honestly, "I was a little uneasy. 'Tis all new to me."

"Indeed it must be. Would you like me to show you about?" He took his hands from his belt and straightened up.

"Aye. I had hoped to find a passageway to the open air. I cannot sleep indoors. I never have."

"Never?" he said again with the same doubt.

"Never," she repeated. "Must I have a man's voice for you to believe me?"

He grinned at that. "Nay, it's just that you are different."

"Truth, I am different from you . . . and you are different from me. Shall we draw swords and fight over our differences?"

Now he laughed outright. "Milady, you are in ill temper."

"That I am," she admitted.

"Do you think that men fight each time they do not agree?"

"From the tales I've heard, it seems so."

His face sobered. "If that is what you believe about men, then I think 'tis your good fortune that I've taken you under my wing—"

She gave him a hard stare and interjected, "It's more the way that you've taken *my* wings."

"Ah . . . so we're back to that already."

"We never left."

He leaned closer, put his hands on her shoulders and said quietly, "Let's leave off for tonight. What say I show you my castle and tell you whatever you wish to know about the world of men . . . and you in turn tell me of the realm of Myr."

Again, he was the paragon of courtliness. He stood so close that for one disturbing moment, Arrah could not answer or even breathe properly. She remained still under his touch, wondering all the while why she felt such excitement at his proximity. Aye, she should ask him. But what if it was just her own nervousness and had nothing to do with him.

She looked at him, at his rugged face and firm lips, his dark eyes warm as firelight; and she felt the strength of his hands on her shoulders and remembered when she had first faced him on the lochshore. Aye, she did want to know more . . . not so much about men, but about him.

"I'm in agreement. Yet . . ." She thought to bargain a little. "If I'm to stay here more than this night, I'll have my chambers be the open air of your courtyard and my pallet on the upper landing of a castle tower."

"You've only to ask, milady." He dropped his hands and gave a slight bow. "Follow me," he requested, and stepped around her. Taking the keys from his waist, he sorted through them and then put one into the lock mouth. The hinges groaned, and the sound caused Arrah's breath to slow a pace.

The candlelight easily exposed a circular chamber with ceiling-high shelves lined with parchment scrolls and a table on which sat glass crockery for the distilling of essences. She supposed it a workroom of sorts. A dank smell seemed to creep toward her like a faint mist, enveloping her in a stifling melancholy. Tears welled in her eyes, and that empathic sense in her knew that this chamber held a profound sorrow within its confines.

She watched him cross the room.

"And what do you think so far?" His words echoed oddly off the chamber walls.

"What do I think of what?" she asked, not following because she was listening more to the unspoken than the spoken.

"Of Rhune Castle." He had opened a small lancet window, and the draw of air caused the candle to go out.

In the same instance, something cold touched the back of her neck. She twirled about, but in the dark saw nothing. Though the presence, whatever it was, did not seem malevolent, her heart was beating at a ferocious pace.

She saw a flash, and soon the room was again aglow with a light that the mage held in his hand. With curiosity, she narrowed the distance between them. In the center of his palm he held a luminous sphere.

"Here, you may hold it."

He put the sphere into her hand. The outside felt cold and soft. "What is it?"

"An ancient taper. I found it in a cave across the loch, where they spawn upon the wall like glass baubles. You've only to rub your hands together and the heat causes it to light. Have you ever seen one in Myr?"

"No. We've faerie lights, but they are different than this."

"It stays alight for many hours. So," he continued, "I'm still wondering what you think of Rhune Castle."

She sighed and began, "'Tis not a pleasant place to be. I had expected more than haunted chambers and dour-faced warriors whose hearts are closed to any measure of feeling."

His features shifted into mock offense. "Not a pleasant place to be? Lady, you insult my Fianna, my person and my abode."

"You asked and I spoke honestly."

"Take a moment to reconsider. Mayhap you were too harsh—"

"—or too honest," she interjected.

He studied her closer, the dark eyes never wavering as he looked.

She returned his gaze steadily, finding herself wholly puzzled. Something about his face held her, something in the lean, irregular features which might be handsome or ugly. There was an uncompromising blend of the two, giving him the appearance of ungentled ruthlessness.

"Have you seen enough?" he finally asked.

Coming to herself, she said, "Forgive me for staring."

"Now we are even," he said with a half-laugh.

She stepped back. "I must confess that this is the only castle I've been inside and that you are the first man I've seen. I have nothing to compare you or the castle with."

"Lady, you make excuses now. I shall let it pass, but in the future be more circumspect in your criticisms."

She was not sure what he meant. "First you tell me

not to question, now not to criticize. Am I to hold my tongue and never speak?"

"Nay, speak as you will, but so none will take offense," he advised.

"'Tis only you who takes offense," she declared.

Something shifted in his features. He did not like her open speaking, for he was used to being in control. She looked at him, at his dark eyes and firm mouth; indeed, his face was as craggy as granite cliffs. Aye, but there was vulnerability in him as well as strength.

Studying him thoughtfully, she remembered asking Terwen about men, and her answer had been, "Each man is a riddle unto himself." Well, she had always loved riddles, and the one standing before her was proving to be challenge enough. Aye, like he had said, he was many men in one.

"I owe you an apology," she amended. "It would be unwise to cause offense, especially to the Mage of the Dragon's Mouth." And then, with a touch of mischief in her voice, she said, "I have no wish to end up a wart on a toad's back."

Her jest dispelled the tension between them.

He smiled at her, and she watched the tiny flames spring to instant life in his eyes. "In truth, you would be the fairest wart that ever appeared upon a toad's back. Come, now, Arrah of Myr, and let me take you for a walk upon the battlements of my castle." He took the sphere from her hand and set it carefully upon a small pedestal.

The mage led her down a short passageway. She was glad to leave the room, for she felt an uneasy presence there. It was haunted. Indeed, all the castle was haunted.

He opened a narrow door that brought them to the tower walk.

"Take your ease, milady," he said with a grand sweep of his arm. "Consider my entire fortress at your disposal—lifeless as it may be."

Ignoring his sarcasm, she breathed in the fresh air and sighed. "Oh, 'tis refreshing after the closeness inside." She leaned out over the parapet and took in the full expanse of the forested mountains and the yawning loch below. "Aye, we're high up!" she exclaimed.

"You cannot be afraid of heights," he said.

"Only when I have no wings." She laughed, and moved across the walkway to see the other side.

He followed her, standing near. "Tell me. . . . What is it like to fly so high one might touch the stars?"

"Do you not know?" She turned her gaze away from the loch and back to him.

He shook his head. " 'Tis not within my ken. In that regard I am more my father's race than my mother's."

"Beway . . ." she began. His words had stunned her. "Until this moment I have never thought about what it would be like not to fly. Did you take my feather skin in hopes of flying yourself?"

He seemed on the verge of laughing, but he did not. "Nay, the thought never entered my mind."

"Then why?"

He scratched his chin. "I'm still wondering myself."

His face was swarthy in the moonlight. He stood looking at her, and slowly the world seemed to recede into the vast and breathless silence of heaven. All faded away—there were no sounds from below, no faint rustle of wind in the trees—and Arrah remembered the strange moment she had first seen him by the loch, when her heart had missed a beat.

He put out his hand and pushed aside a wayward lock of hair beside her cheek. She did not move, for all will had left her at his touch. Then he held her chin and lifted her face to his.

"I'm told there is bewitchment in the kiss of a swan maiden," he said quietly.

" 'Tis true," she answered, low.

"That is the pity. If not, I would kiss you."

She wanted his kiss as she had never wanted anything before. For that kiss she would have ransomed not only her swan skin, but her soul.

His hand dropped to his side and he took a step back. "Come, there is more to see. Where to first? You may choose. The stables, kitchen or armory? Wherever your fancy leads."

Her fancy led to his face; the only place she wished to explore was his mouth. But she dared not say it. "Take me where you wish. I'll follow."

He put out his hand to take hers.

They walked along the battlement together, and he did not release his hold. Arrah knew in some way that he had captured more than her feather skin and that she must go wherever that strong hand led, no matter what befell her.

"Rhune Castle is very ancient. None know how it was built or by whom. Mayhap it grew out of granite rock through sorcery," he said as they approached the adjacent tower. "Three towers form its heart. There's the tower of the dragon's claw, the one we just left." He pointed behind them. "Then there's the tower of the dragon's fire, beyond . . . and here before us is the tower of the dragon's fang."

Arrah turned her head to glimpse the towers. All three were connected by the battlement walkways and loomed darkly above them.

"In my childhood, I lived here alone, yet I do not fully know its every step and corridor. Rooms come and go. Doorways often disappear. Within its bowels, 'tis ever changing."

"Does anyone become lost?"

"All the time. 'Tis a hazard of living here. But none have come to harm, and most are the better for the adventure." He opened the tower door for her to pass through. "If you find yourself lost, the secret is to always climb an upward path and keep taking any intersect of corridor marked by the twining dragon heads."

Still holding her hand, he began down the spiral stairs. She near lost her balance, not being used to steps, especially when taken so quickly.

"Hold tight, take three steps at a time and trust me not to let you fall. I'll show you *my* way of flying," he chuckled.

She did as he asked. Down, down he leaped ahead of her, his footsteps swift, ever on the edge, but never out of control. It was not long before she became dizzy, her feet merely dusting the steps. Suddenly, he let go of her hand and caught her up upon his back. Faster and faster, he carried her downward on his broad shoulders. Excitement washed over her. She liked the feel and vibrancy of him.

She saw the door coming head-on and squealed aloud. But he halted short. She was breathless and he was laughing as he dropped her to her feet.

Her knees buckled, but he caught her in his arms and held her close to him. Trying not to fall, she leaned into him. He felt hard and soft at once. Her cheek brushed against his; his skin chafed hers. Aye, it was rough like bark or sandstone. Pulling back, she lifted her fingers to explore his chin, then irrepressibly, she traced his lips.

His eyes locked upon hers and his large hand captured her fingers. "I'm not a green lad. You'll not seduce me with your netherworld charms and bewitchments." Then he grinned as his thumb nuzzled open her fingers and he touched a soft kiss to her palm.

He might as well have breathed fire into her, for the heat of his kiss traversed into her very heart. In the beginning by the loch she had not chosen him, but now . . .

"Come, you shall meet the Fianna and see the great

hall." He sidestepped away from her and shouldered open the door.

She did not move at first—she could not. So much in her was a tremble of emotion and fire and wanting. . . . Now, she understood why she was discontent in Myr and what had driven her out into the world of men this midsummer's eve. It was Traeth of Rhune, the Mage of the Dragon's Mouth, she'd come to find.

"Don't be frightened, the Fianna are harmless in their own lair."

She did not believe him, but stepped through the threshold into the anteroom that was a transit passage between the hall and the spiral stair.

Talking ceased and heads turned when she and Traeth entered the hall. Still breathless, she was scarcely ready to be appraised by a roomful of curious men. Some were playing a dice game on the floor before the hearth, and a dozen or so others lounged about polishing scabbards and shields.

Arrah's eyes widened. Hearths in the shape of giant, stone dragons flanked each end of the hall. A smoldering fire burned in each gaping mouth. Tapestries hung on the walls above swords, shields and other weaponry of battle. A shiver crept down her spine when she spied human and animal skulls placed about the hall as lanterns. *Beway,* she thought, *they must drink the blood of their enemies from the silver goblets lining the tables.*

"My Fianna," Traeth said. "I present to you the lady Arrah of Myr."

Parting themselves from the others, two men, dressed much like Traeth in leather tunics and leggings, came forward and bowed.

"I am Dath Bright Spear," said one. Arrah was fascinated by the black, braided beard hanging like a long tail from his chin.

"Our enemies have offered a bounty of gold for the

head and fine beard of Dath Bright Spear," said Traeth.

"'Tis a gruesome thing for them to do," said Arrah, unabashedly.

"I agree, milady," said Dath, bestowing a flashing smile upon her.

The other called himself Enwir, Malicious in Battle. He looked very fierce indeed. His muscled arms hung by his sides like two great clubs.

Carne the Aged stepped from behind Enwir and took her hand. "I am honored once again, lady swan," he said.

"Do not be misled by his good manners," warned Traeth. "He's the canniest old wizard within the five kingdoms when it comes to guile and craft."

"I do believe you," agreed Arrah, but she smiled as she said it.

"And there is Fergus Dry Lips, a scoundrel's scoundrel," Traeth said, moving on. "And before the hearth you must not miss Camlan the Unsmiling. He is the heartthrob of every maid who lays eyes upon him," declared Traeth.

It was not Camlan the Unsmiling who caught Arrah's eye, but the crouching form at his feet. Her heart leaped. Sib! There was her sister Sib.

In the moment their eyes locked in recognition, Traeth said, "And here is another vagabond of this enchanted night. I cannot say from where or why she's come. But she shadows our Camlan with more devotion than a hound in heat."

Neither she nor Sib dared say a word. Arrah realized that the worst had happened. In the most vulnerable of phases before chrysalis, Sib had encountered the man Camlan and imprinted on him. This meant her heart, her fealty and her person would be wholly fixated on Camlan. Everywhere he went she would follow. Such a bonding was rare, because most swan maidens never left Myr to encounter men until after chrysalis. She would be his servant or slave . . . whatever he chose. He had no need to capture her feather skin.

Camlan the Unsmiling was not without gallantry, and he gave Arrah a slight bow. However, she saw no compassion in his handsome face for little Sib. He considered her a nuisance, to be sure, and at her wretched stage of life she would be.

"She might serve as lady's maid to you, if we can pry her from Camlan's heels," offered Traeth.

"Aye! I will need a friend here," said Arrah, so quickly that Traeth's eyes narrowed quizzically.

She walked over to the hearth and stooped down on bent knee. "Did you hear? The mage says you are to be with me now."

Sib frowned at her.

Arrah came very close to scolding her outright. It was no time for her to be stubborn. "'Tis for your own good," she said.

Sib looked away.

In her innocence, Sib had no idea of the predicament she'd put herself into. The sooner they escaped the better. Yet Arrah knew that escape was far from Sib's mind.

Mayhap it was her own frayed nerves, or Sib's undisguised stubbornness, but Arrah was in no mood to beg or plead. "You come with me," she insisted.

"Do you not hear?" said Camlan, reaching out his fingers and catching Sib in an ear pinch. He pulled her to her feet and with a cuff on the side of her head thrust her toward Arrah. "Go with her!" he ordered.

Traeth protested, "Now, don't be too heavy-handed with her."

Arrah was taken back by Camlan's meanness. He had struck her sister. She stood very still and glared at him. He returned her stare, and she felt his contempt like a tangible thing. Not intimidated by his arrogance, she gave him one last look, then turned back to Sib.

"Aye," said Fergus, "she may bite."

"She'll not bite me," assured Arrah. "I've a way with such creatures."

Hurtfully, like a faithful hound that had just been kicked by its master, Sib continued to look at Camlan.

"Come along. 'Tis for your own good," Arrah muttered under her breath.

Sib's eyes were watering.

Fully entertained by the sight, the Fianna were making jests as Arrah pushed her out of the hall to the spiral stairway.

"What shall you do with her?" asked Traeth.

"I shall keep her by my side until she comes to her senses. 'Tis the only way. Good night to you," she called over her shoulder. "I shall resume my explorations tomorrow."

"I'll have a servant bring you sleeping pallets," returned Traeth after her. Amusement marked his voice. "You can fall asleep as is your wont, beneath the stars . . . beside your new companion."

Once within the cold confines of the tower stairs, Arrah turned to Sib. "Now stay with me!" she commanded, her irritation rising high. "You've gotten us in enough trouble for one night."

"Me?" cried Sib. "'Twas you who brought me here."

"I did not tell you to fly over the loch and spy upon the castle. That was your own doing."

"But you did bring me. You wanted to come yourself. And I think you were more curious than me. How did you come here?"

"I came because the Mage of the Dragon's Mouth captured my feather skin while I waited for you!"

"So you blame me for that as well," gasped Sib.

"No," sighed Arrah, trying to gather patience. "I don't blame you for that as well. I left it unguarded and will take the responsibility of it." Then she stopped midstep. "Where is your feather skin?"

"'Tis hidden outside the castle."

"Does Camlan know?"

"Camlan . . ." Sib repeated his name wistfully. "Don't you think he is handsome?"

"I cannot judge," returned Arrah shortly. "And how could you believe someone who has just slapped you is handsome?"

"Truly, he did not mean to."

"Truly, he did or he would not have slapped you." Arrah clicked her tongue with disgust. "Now forget your Camlan and be serious. Does he know you are a swan maiden?"

"Nay, he thinks I'm the ugly spawn of a forest spriggan."

"Well, that is in our favor at least."

"Why do you say that?"

"Because he would entrap you here like the mage has entrapped me."

"I would not mind," smiled Sib, her eyes so glazed with fancy that Arrah felt like slapping her herself, just to snap her out of the delusion.

"I want you to leave the castle, recover your swan feathers and fly back into Myr."

"Leave Camlan?"

"Aye, leave Camlan!"

"Never!" Sib stopped short on the stair and crossed her arms before her flat chest in defiance.

"Can't you see, he cares not a whit for you," declared Arrah.

"Then I shall wait until I transform. When he sees me then, I'll be beautiful and he'll love me."

"Beauty should make no difference. If he loves you for how you look then 'tis no love at all. Now, come on . . . we haven't all night," said Arrah, pulling her forward.

"Then, I shall kiss him and he will be hopelessly enchanted."

"That is worse, for when the enchantment wears off he'll scorn you. No, in matters of love 'tis better to leave off the magicks and bewitchments," advised Arrah.

"But I love him," said Sib, her wide eyes filling with great tears.

"Nay, you love the idea of love. You are in love with love," Arrah said, feeling as though she should admonish herself as well. "We are a foolish pair. We leave the safe haven of Myr and the first men we see, we think we are in love with them."

They had come to the door that opened onto the battlement walk. Against Sib's mild protests, Arrah nudged her along and through the door of the tower of the dragon's fang.

"Where are we going?" asked Sib, sniveling.

"I want to return to the chamber and see if you are clever enough to open the trunk where the mage has put my swan skin. If you can, then we will both leave this dark place and be done with our adventure."

"I'm not ready for my adventure to be done."

Arrah did not answer, but pushed her onward and down the wind of stairs. She wanted nothing more than to escape this castle and its dark enchantments. She feared that soon she would be as smitten with Traeth of Rhune as Sib was with Camlan the Unsmiling.

"Sib, 'tis the way of our kind to love too well. We are both too inexperienced in a realm where men bury their feelings and deny their hearts. We must leave."

"You leave—I'm not going to," announced Sib firmly. "How are we to get experience if we run away? Isn't that why we came?"

"No, we came because . . ." Arrah's voice wavered; she wasn't being wholly honest.

". . . Because you wanted to see a man. You told me so. And now you are afraid," concluded Sib.

"Aye, I'm afraid. But so would you be if a man captured your swan feathers."

They had come to a threshold. "Take the passage of the twining dragons," Arrah told Sib. The passage looked strange, and she realized that in the short time since she'd left everything had subtly changed. They passed many doors, until Arrah recognized the one of the frowning tree spirit.

"Here," she said to Sib with deep relief. What if she had never found the chamber again? She would never have found her feather skin either. She pulled the latch and the door swung open. "There," she pointed, "in that chest against the wall is my feather skin. The chest is locked. The mage wears the key with others about his waist, so there is slim chance of me taking it."

Sib walked over and knelt down beside the chest. She examined the lock and then turned to Arrah. "'Tis odd the lengths men go to keep things from each other. Did you see the great drawbridge that they raise and lower to keep themselves in and others out? That would never do in Myr."

Beside her Arrah agreed. "Aye, in Myr there would be no reason for a drawbridge."

"I think this can be opened by an air charm," said Sib, taking a deep breath and puffing three times into the mouth of the lock.

Arrah heard a click. "'Twas so simple, I wonder why they bother to take such device," she said.

Sib lifted the lid and peered inside. Arrah leaned over her shoulder, her eyes searching for a glimpse of her swan skin.

The longer Sib rummaged through the contents, the more anxiety gripped Arrah.

"'Tis not here," Sib finally said.

"But I saw him put it in," said Arrah, pushing Sib

out of the way and reaching in herself. Frantically, she tossed things aside.

With a despairing sigh, she said, "'Tis no use. He must have moved it. Or tricked me with illusion." She came to her feet.

"Now what will you do?" asked Sib.

"I will do nothing less than search this castle from the tower top to the dungeon bottom."

"That might take some time," said Sib, her face brightening.

"I know what you are thinking." She pointed her finger at Sib. "By my order you will stay away from Camlan the Unsmiling. He is a heartbreaker."

"'Tis my heart," returned Sib, her face defiant.

"Aye, 'tis your heart all right, and it will be your aching. I mean only to protect you in this realm of men. You have heard the stories our sisters have told." Arrah sighed. "But I know you are not one to learn from secondhand experience. When you are moaning and wasting away from the pain, do not expect any consolation from me, but an 'I told you so.' Now come along. I am tired and wish to rest." Arrah turned to leave the room and climb to the open air of the battlewalk.

"I don't believe you have a heart," said Sib, dragging behind her.

"Believe what you will. I'm thinking that it would be an advantage not to have one."

Once out upon the battlement walk, again she heard the lilting music of a harp. It was not within the castle walls, but faint upon the breeze whispering from the loch. The feather pallets Traeth had promised were stacked against the wall. Together she and Sib arranged them neatly and lay down.

Gazing into the dark heaven, she let loose a long sigh. "'Tis all enchantment of midsummer's eve. Mayhap when we wake at morning's light, 'twill all be a dream."

"Humph," grumbled Sib. "I hope not. I like it here. In Myr everything is the same—the weather, the food, the gossip. Did you see the sword at Camlan's hip? I would like to have a sword like that."

"And what would you do with one? You could not take it back to Myr."

"I would ride at Camlan's side in battle," she declared.

"Och, next you'll be telling me that you wish to join the ranks of the Morrigan."

"Who are the Morrigan?" Sib perked with interest.

"The warrior queens. They teach the art of war to young men and eat the bodies of the battle dead. Carne the Aged told me that the mage was taught the arts of war by them in his youth."

"Do they only teach men?"

"Sib, 'twould be against your nature. Besides, you could not return to Myr, for no one harboring the heart or weapons of war can travel the ley path into that realm. Now, go to sleep and cease thinking of it."

"If I could deftly wield a sword, Camlan would love me better," she rattled on.

"No, he would love you less. A man does not like a woman who can outdo him."

"Why not?"

"Men like to be the best at whatever they do."

"Och," breathed Sib, raising herself on one elbow to look at Arrah. "So do I."

Arrah could not help but giggle at her sister's quandary.

Sib lay back again, staring up at the sky.

Arrah lay motionless, wondering how either of them would be served by remaining in the realm of men. She was afraid.

She had never been afraid of anything before. . . .

Chapter

And do you sleep until noon in your land of Myr?"

Still caught in the grasps of sleep, Arrah squinted into the gray light of morning. Whose voice was that? So deep and teasing.

"I dare not kiss you to awaken you as they do in the old tales. You'll have to settle for a sponge of cold water on your face, milady."

Slowly, awareness was coming back to her. Aye, that voice belonged to Traeth of Rhune. A sinking feeling gripped her stomach as she realized her capture, the castle and Sib lying beside her were not just parts of a bad dream.

She sat up and through the haze saw him half-kneeling before her. "The sun's . . ." she began in a croak. She had to pause to clear her throat. Then, trying once more, she said, "The sun's not up. 'Tis yet the middle of the night."

"I've come to take you riding so we can see the sunrise together."

She looked at him, his dark hair smoothed, his mouth poised between laughter and seriousness, and wondered if he was set on torturing her. Aye, to awaken her at this early hour was torture.

"'Tis not my habit to awaken with the birds," she said flatly, and curled back down.

"That's surprising, milady swan," he said, a little too glibly.

Her rising irritation wiped away the last vestige of sleepiness. She sat up again. Pushing hair away from her eyes, she met his gaze. Slowly, she said, "I may be of the swan clan, but if 'tis morning twittering you want, catch yourself a warbler."

He laughed outright, and the soft tinkle of Sib's mirth joined in the sound. Arrah cast her sister a shushing glance.

Then, with some impatience, he stood upright. "Now dress yourself and come along or we will miss sunrise altogether."

Arrah frowned, but knew when she was bested. She reached for the tunic and leggings she'd discarded during the night because they were too rough to sleep in. Within minutes, he was leading her down the tower of the dragon's claw and out into the courtyard.

"Can you ride?" he asked when they approached two white destriers awaiting them before the castle gates.

"Aye, we've unicorns and winged horses in Myr," she replied, stroking the long silken mane of one horse.

"Those animals I would indeed like to see." He cupped his hands and boosted her into the high saddle.

"That you never will, for such creatures are too smart to venture out into your world of men."

"And what does that say about yourself?" he asked, mounting his horse.

"It says what I belatedly know: I was foolish, and more foolish to leave my swan skin unguarded for the likes of you to steal. My sis—" she continued, then quickly corrected herself. "I returned to my chamber and to the trunk where I saw you put my swan skin. 'Tis no longer there."

"How did you open the lock?" he asked.

"I have my ways."

"That I'm discovering," he chuckled.

She persisted. "Where is my feather skin? You do not have the right to keep it."

He was no longer smiling, but neither were his eyes distant. "What is right and wrong in Myr is not necessarily what is right and wrong in the borderlands. You came for adventure, and you shall have it to your fill and more, milady. When you crossed over from Myr you chose a path. Mayhap that is what divides the realms faerie and men—free choice. Once an adventure begins and the choice is made, there is no turning back until it's ridden through."

Arrah fell silent, knowing in her heart that what he said was true. Had she not crossed over she would have never discovered the riddle of man, or the manner of man before her. She would never have seen the restless beauty of the Loch of the Dragon's Mouth and the mystery of Rhune Castle. Aye, she had no choice but to ride the adventure through until she regained her swan skin and her freedom.

He lightened, and she watched the tiny flames dance in his eyes. "Come away, Arrah of Myr, and begin your adventure." He kneed his horse ahead, and hers obediently followed.

The mountains rose against the changing sky of dawn, one behind the other as far as the eye could see. High on a precipice overlooking the loch, he halted so that she might look her fill. She watched in spellbound delight as the sun crested the mountain peak and flashed in a shimmer of gold on the surface of the water.

Almost worshipfully, she watched the sun suffuse the sky with colors as vivid as any she had seen in the morning mists of Myr. " 'Tis worth waking for," she confessed.

"Each day dawns but once," he said, his gaze resting on some intangible point in the distance.

Arrah thought his words very sagacious, but then Terwen had told her that men were very philosophical. Terwen had once said, "Men's main occupation is killing one another in well-planned and not so well-planned ways. Then, they sit before the fire drinking mead and justifying their violence through philosophy."

Although Arrah noted the sheathed dagger at the mage's waist, in the fresh light of sunrise he did not appear murderous in the slightest. A part of her hoped he'd never killed anyone, but another part of her knew he had. She had seen the lack of innocence in every face of the Fianna. When a man killed, he wore that deed in his features—a dark line here, a wrinkle there. Terwen had said that when a man killed often, viciously and for the lust of it, his eyes became flat and dead. Arrah hoped she would never meet such a man.

Taking the reins of his horse, Traeth asked, "Would you like a morning swim?"

Arrah grinned openly at the thought. "I can think of nothing better. You lead and I will follow."

He took a track that was rough and steep as it continued along the uplands. Gaunt hills, wild moors and rock-littered gorges surrounded them. He began to descend in a direct line through green trees and hidden glens. A stream, bordered by green bracken and clumps of fern, meandered its lazy course along the ground and disappeared into a stand of slender trees. Beyond the trees the slopes opened to a bright wedge of blue that was the Loch of the Dragon's Mouth.

" 'Tis a wild and beautiful place," she said.

"Not only wild and beautiful, but the best hiding place in the five kingdoms."

"I can't think why you would find it needful to hide."

"The reasons a man sometimes must absent himself from the world and its affairs is not for you to question."

"Are women never to question in the realm of men?"

"Aye, a woman may question, but she must be sure her man has the answer."

"That is silly. I think there are some questions that have no answers."

"In that you are right," he agreed with a faint smile.

"Suppose I have a question for you. How do I know whether you have the answer unless I ask the question?"

"I admit there is a certain risk." He moved his horse slowly down the slope, leading the way.

"Are you a man of disrepute in the five kingdoms? Is that why you must hide here?"

He was silent for a lengthy interval.

Arrah remained puzzled, and wondered if she had asked a question he could not answer and if now he would never speak to her again.

Finally, he said, "I do not hide here, I live here. But to speak truly, I do have enemies. You do know what enemies are, don't you?"

"Aye, but in Myr everyone likes everyone, so I myself have no enemies."

"You do now. My enemies are your enemies. That is how it works here in the realm of men."

"But why should that be?"

"Because you dwell at Rhune Castle. Look at it as if you belong to my clan."

"Your clan is a warrior clan. I am no warrior."

"But you are a warrior's woman."

"Hah! 'Tis only you who thinks so. I am my own woman," she said with defiance.

"As long as I hold your swan skin, you are my woman," he replied just as firmly.

It was Arrah's turn to be silent. He could be so companionable, then so unyielding.

They rode on down the hillside, over sunlit green meadows and beside the sparkling stream. Outwardly all appeared peaceful, but inside Arrah was churning like a sea in high storm. It was as if he had his hand around her very neck, choking away her breath along with her freedom. She did not like this realm of men where a woman held no place of her own.

At last he turned in the saddle and gave her a sidelong scrutiny. "Did you know your eyes turn as red as rubies when you are angry?"

Caught unawares, she stared at him as if he were daft.

"Nay," he said thoughtfully, " 'tis more the color of the sky at sunset, or mayhap a hearth fire when the snow is deep and the night long."

A part of her wanted to retreat in panic from the incalculable power of his words to expose her anger and then send her reeling toward heaven.

"Why don't you speak your anger?" he asked suddenly. "Give me a few sharp words."

She had a myriad of sharp words for him, but she bit her lip and kept her silence.

"Is anger not allowed in a land as peaceful as Myr? How do you settle your disputes?"

His question was not unreasonable. Arrah answered in short reply. "We molt."

"You molt?"

"Aye, every so often we molt. 'Tis a shedding and rebirth process where we let everything go . . . including our feathers. The anger and other emotions are returned to the earth to be transformed."

"Bedad!" He laughed heartily.

"You are laughing at me."

"No, no, not at you," he denied in a feeble attempt to gather himself.

"Then why do you laugh if 'tis not at me?"

"I'm imagining myself molting away my anger. 'Tis an extreme way to befuddle one's enemies. In my mind's eye I see a battlefield of flying feathers and squawking warriors."

"We don't squawk," she said, her tolerance of him thinning.

"You are too serious. I was merely jesting," he chuckled. "Women are damnably sensitive. You'll not go weepy on me, will you?"

"I'm not weepy." Indeed, she was far from crying.

"Good. I only said it to rid you of that sulky pout."

"I'm neither sulking nor pouting," she said crisply. "'Tis only . . ."

"'Tis only that you have never fully experienced such emotions before. During your stay here you might find a greater understanding for the likes of we mortal men. Would that I could molt away my anger, or any other strong emotion that breaks my discontent."

He brought the horses to a halt, then rested his arm on his saddle pommel and gave her so speculative a look that her cheeks burned. "The beauty and serenity of Myr may be the stuff of legends, but in Myr you were only partly alive. You are hungering for something more, or you would never have ventured forth from that safe haven. In this realm of men you will feel every thrust of anger, every tear of grief and every pang of your heart. 'Tis the way of men to live life fully embodied."

"It may be the way of men, but I am a woman and 'tis not my way." She fixed him with a haughty stare. "I want my swan skin, so that I may leave this realm of men."

"No."

Arrah stiffened. The word was a cold spear aimed at her very breast. It was a no that meant no. How could he flatly refuse to return to her what she most wanted?

"We must leave the horses here," he said, dismounting, "and trust to our feet the remainder of the way."

When he offered his hand to her she did not take it, but remained on her horse, glowering.

"Do you intend to sit there and molt away your dander?"

Her blood rose at his blatant disregard and a sudden she felt as mad as a bogey in daylight.

"Milady?" He continued to hold out his hand and she continued to simmer.

"Milady, your eyes are still red fire and the tips of your ears are turning crimson," he observed. "You've something to say, so speak up. Holding it in will only give you colic."

Inwardly fomenting, she glared at him until she thought her chin would break from the strain. She knew her eyes must be bright as twin coals under a cooking pot. Indeed, she would have gladly given him a slice of her anger, but the lump of wrath choking her throat left her mute. Never had she felt such an eruption of overwhelming emotion. And what vexed her most was his good humor through it all.

She felt the sting of tears in her eyes. The last thing she wanted to do was cry, but how else could she release the emotion festering in her if she could not molt?

Suddenly, it released itself in a burst of hiccups and tears. She found her voice and sniveled out inanely, "Don't think to—*hiccup*—bully me. I come from a peaceful race—*hiccup* . . ."

He listened, hands on his hips, watching her with a faint, inscrutable smile on his face. After her last hiccup he said, "Then let us have peace between us, milady swan."

"Truly, that is what I've wanted all along, but you, a warrior, know nothing of peace," she sniffed.

"I know fear is an enemy to peace."

His words stunned her. Until this moment she'd never thought about fear, mainly because fear did not exist in Myr, only love.

So, the problem with the realm of men was that men had strayed from love. Here fear seemed more real than love. Mayhap, she thought, that was what happened so long ago when the two realms divided: Those who remained in Myr chose love and the others veered into fear. And now she herself was fearful, for living in this realm she was beginning to believe fear's illusion.

"Wherever there is fear in the five kingdoms, the warrior is needed," Traeth spoke on, justifying himself.

Hiccups under control, she took a deep breath and felt better. She did not wait for him to help her off her horse, but slipped down herself and countered, "But the warrior breeds fear."

"Aye, but only to the fearful."

Her lips pursed with perplexity. Surely men and women did not reason the same.

"Your cheeks are damp, milady." With his fingers, he gently wiped away the last vestige of tears. "Now, don't you feel better?"

She nodded, for she did. Although nothing much was settled between them, her temper had cooled.

The stream had disappeared in a tangle of gorse that presented an impenetrable barrier across their path. With characteristic agility he climbed over the face of a great boulder and reached down to give her a hand up. Reluctantly, she placed her own small hand in his and scrambled up after him. He led her along the edge of a precipice and down the opposite face to a rocky slope rising to the right of the drop-off. There he held aside the underbrush, and a clear path appeared. The trail led downward, twisting among the boulders, and she felt his hand on her arm to steady her on the rough ground. Still angry with him, she did not want his touch. Yet, at the same time, a part of her melted under its warmth.

At the bottom of the incline, she stood beside him in a small glen, surrounded by steep hillsides and trees whose leaves shimmered in the morning sunlight like emeralds. A carpet of fragrant wildflowers, moss and meadow grass felt soft against her feet after the rocky downward path. The stream surged frothily down the rock face into a waterfall and formed a small pool before rushing to the loch beyond.

" 'Tis a lovely spot," she had to admit.

"Aye, I thought you would like it. I believe 'tis the closest thing to Myr in the borderlands. I've known men who come here once and never wish to leave."

"No wonder," she said, pointing to a circle of scarlet toadstools. "It belongs to the faeries. They've left their mark and have cast their spell."

"And what spell would that be?" he asked, smiling with whimsy.

"The spell of love, of course," she said, relaxing into the magic of the spot.

"Do faeries know any other spells?" he asked, dropping to the ground and stretching his long legs out before him.

"Aye, they do. But faeries on the whole are mischievous and take the most delight in causing as much havoc as possible. Certainly, nothing does that more than love."

"True," he agreed.

She strolled to the edge of the pool and sat down on a flat stone. It was clear to its peat-brown depths. It sparkled with sunlight and flecks of white froth from the falling water.

"Take your swim," he said.

She turned to see him put his hands behind his head

and look up at the sky. She needed no more words of encouragement, and in seconds she had slipped from her tunic and leggings. It felt more natural for her to be unclothed than clothed.

Traeth watched her long, graceful limbs ease out of her garments. She stretched her arms skyward and gave a freeing sigh. Her long, thick hair gleamed like polished gold and her fair skin shone white as alabaster. Then, he lowered his eyes, aggravated at his response to her naked beauty. An instinctual sense of self-preservation told him he should return her swan skin and send her back to Myr. How long could he resist her her bewitchments? How long before he kissed those lips and gave up *his* freedom to *her?*

Again his gaze strayed to her as she stepped into the pool. Her head turned to him and flashed an innocent but undeniable invitation to join her.

"'Tis not cold," she called.

He watched the perfect curve of her smooth hips lower into the water. Between one breath and the next, he surrendered to his need.

He pulled off his boots and leathers. Then, naked, he walked toward the pool.

He felt her eyes upon him. There was nothing discreet about her open perusal. He knew she'd never seen the full form of a man before, and he was content to allow her full view of his masculinity.

"'Tis unbelievably cold," he gasped as his foot touched the icy water.

"I thought you, the Mage of the Dragon's Mouth, would be used to swimming in frigid mountain streams."

"Unlike you, I do not have a natural affinity to water, nor do I like the cold. Count it as one of my weaknesses."

"Terwen says that to do anything we do not wish to do builds character."

"My character is strong enough," he retorted, carefully easing himself into the water. "Who is Terwen?" He bore the scrotum-numbing shock bravely.

Arrah moved away from him to the far end of the pool. "She is my guardian. Much like Carne the Aged is to you."

His curiosity piqued, he asked, "Has she ventured into the world of men?"

"Many times."

"What did she tell you about men?"

"That they are riddles even to themselves."

"True," he acquiesced, sinking shoulder high into the water. "But are you not a riddle to yourself?"

"Aye, that I am. I suppose the mystery of self is a never-ending adventure to explore."

The lapping of water over the swell of her full breasts momentarily captured his gaze. "What did she say about men and women together?" he asked lazily.

Her eyes twinkled. "She said, and I quote: 'When a man and woman fall in love, they both fall in love with *him.*'"

Traeth grinned. "You swan maidens are incorrigible."

"Indeed, we are different from the women in your realm. We speak our mind and bow to no man. We are bonded in strength, and the power of that unity holds our world apart from yours."

"Aye, yours is an ancient lineage, more ancient than that of my mother. She was a Tuatha woman." He had never brought this up before with anyone, and now wished he hadn't.

"Carne told me of your history," she said quietly. "Why did your mother leave your father?"

"I do not know. Mayhap she was a wild thing like yourself and untamable." He shifted, turning his back on her.

She was not put off. She moved up behind him. "Do you remember your father?"

He did not answer. Then he felt the soft touch of her hand suddenly upon his shoulder. He could not recall when a woman's touch had so affected him. In a natural motion, her fingers massaged the length of muscle to the nape of his neck. There she gathered the loose strands of his hair, wringing the water from the tips.

A lengthy interval passed as she gently continued her ministering. She finally said, "'Tis rare for we swan maidens to know our fathers. When the time for mating is right, we travel the ley path into the world of men. As you know, the first kiss between a man and swan maiden leaves the man hopelessly enchanted by her beauty."

"Hmmm," he said evenly. "Does this enchantment work both ways?"

She crooked her head thoughtfully a moment. "You have asked me a question I cannot answer. I've never kissed a man, so I cannot say."

"Never?" he replied with mock dismay.

"If you think that crossing back and forth between the two worlds and kissing men is all swan maidens have to do, you are mightily mistaken," she said, a little huffy.

"You mean you do other things?" he said in careless sally.

"Of course we do other things. We tend the forest and lake. We fly and swim and raise our daughters. We sing, dance . . . and live."

"It sounds very dull to me," he confessed. "No wonder you crossed into the world of men for excitement."

"Myr is not dull," she defended. "'Tis bliss."

"'Bliss'?" he echoed, not wholly convinced. "So," he continued, "if you have never kissed a man, what makes you think you can enchant one on first kiss?"

She gave him a puzzled look. "I'm not sure. Would

63

you like to kiss me and see?" Her eyes widened innocently, and light speared the glowing filaments of her irises.

He chuckled. "I don't relish being the proof of the pudding, milady. However, I would consent to give you some guidance in the nature of a kiss—without kissing you."

"Is that possible?" Her shyness dissipated and an impish mischief crossed her features.

"Aye," he said. Lifting his hand from the water, he held it in front of her. "Hold up your thumb and forefinger, thusly. Imagine them to be a pair of lips."

She did this, eyeing her fingers studiously.

"Now, you must close your eyes, and your mouth as well." He closed his eyes. "It is most important to understand that there are different sorts of kisses. There are friendly kisses, passionate kisses, kisses of good-bye and hello . . . wet kisses, dry kisses, soggy kisses—"

"—enchanted kisses," she interjected.

"Aye," he smiled, "enchanted kisses, too. After you've chosen what sort of kiss you want to kiss, open your lips, just so, relax your jaw and . . ." He lowered his mouth to his hand and kissed, comically thrusting his tongue like a wagging tail between his fingers.

She had begun to grin, and when he did this, she dissolved into an irresistible fit of giggles. He laughed as well.

"Now you've had your lesson, milady. I shall expect nothing less than perfection if ever you kiss me."

"That's all?" she quizzed, still quivering with laughter.

"That's all to the art of kissing. But the art of lovemaking requires greater skill."

"With swan maidens 'tis the same. There can be more to loving than a brief mating. Tales tell that sometimes the love between a man and a swan maiden can run so deep and strong that when a maiden sings her love lilt she can bond the two for life and beyond death."

"'Tis a romantic notion." He let his gaze play lightly over the velvet of her eyebrows and lashes, then over her lips, with their delicate softness. They stared into each other's eyes for a long time. His awareness of her nakedness so near his own was acute. He wanted to embrace her, to kiss her and taste for himself that sweet elixir of enchantment. But he withheld himself, saying, "For me I would not chose love, for like all magic it has a dark side. My father wasted away with what the Tuatha call the sickness of 'love in absence.'"

For his own good, he moved away from her to the pool's edge and lifted himself up on to the mossy bank.

"Are you afraid that will happen to you?" she asked, her eyes wide.

"Nay, it will not. Though you are a mischievous sprite, be warned that I have tricks of my own. . . . We should go back now."

She frowned. "I would happily live here rather than Rhune Castle."

"No doubt you could, but I would like you by my side, and not paddling about a pool, but on dry land. I am not such a duck as you."

He crushed the urge to catch her golden hair, which floated in a tangle upon the shimmering pool. He stood up, and she reluctantly followed him. Still naked, he stretched full length on the ground and prepared to dry himself in the sun before dressing.

She sat on a boulder beside him. Silence fell between them, and then he heard her voice, so softly that at first the sound was no louder than the song of a linnet off somewhere in the trees. Then a melody emerged, slow and sweet. He lay in the sun and closed his eyes, and was filled with a fine content. She was a woman of many moods and humors, he thought, with so wild a nature that there was surely no way in all the world he could keep her by his side without the capture of her swan skin.

And if I am not careful, he admonished himself, *I will find that she has put a spell on me without a kiss. . . .*

Arrah sat in the sun and watched Traeth sleep. She could not take her gaze off him. Light and shadow danced over the sculpted contours of his naked body. Full of wonder, she regarded him, running her eyes over his wide shoulders and the tangle of damp, thick hair that dusted his muscled shoulders. Her scrutiny followed the narrow hips to the prow of his manhood. A strange yearning tingled through her.

She pulled her eyes up and looked only at his face. As if she had touched him, he opened his eyes to hers and watched her with a probing intentness. In the morning light his eyes were as black as obsidian. The desire in them was almost visible. Her pulse sprinted.

He rose up on one elbow. "Come here," he invited.

A voice inside warned her not to go to him. Once he tasted her love, the voice said, he would never allow her to be free; he would bind her heart as well as her swan skin.

She ignored the warning and slipped off the boulder and down to his side. His hand cupped her face gently, and he looked deep into her eyes. She touched his face, feeling the warmth and rough texture of his cheek. She felt his hand slide down, over her shoulder, lower, to close gently around her breast. The power of that touch stunned her and commanded every part of her to yield to him—to yield to that power that could kill as well as cherish. Terwen once told her that a swan maiden might sleep with a man to take the war out of him. Then, Arrah had not understood, but now, in this moment, she did. In the midst of love, there could be no war.

"Your eyes shine like twin stars . . . my faerie goddess," he whispered. His thumb strolled and dallied around the budding spire of her breast. All the while, sensation jolted through her like the shock of a thunderstorm.

Suddenly, his hand dropped and he pulled back. "We must go," he said.

He stood up, moving with such careless strength that she was reminded of the lithe resilience of a winged stallion. But she saw something else—cunning, calculated to a fine degree. He could war and wound, love and tease, with equal, and deadly, grace.

Her cheeks burned as she donned her leggings and tunic. He had played with her. He had opened the feast hall door, let her see the table spread and then shut it in her face.

Even so, strangely, she was reluctant to leave. The morning had passed too swiftly, and she wished to stay in the hidden glen, with its sun-dappled pool and scarlet toadstools.

He gave her his hand and pulled her to her feet.

"Don't be sad, milady swan," he said. "We will return another time."

"So that you may tease me once again? I think not."

He lifted a dark brow. "You did not like your swim?"

"I did."

"What is it, then?"

His smile disappeared, and his face seemed almost swarthy in the shadows of the trees.

She could not answer. He stood looking at her, and suddenly the world seemed to recede like mist from a morning meadow, leaving behind an exposing, breathless silence.

Then he put out his hand and pushed a wayward lock of hair off her forehead. She did not move, could not, as he held her chin and lifted her face to his.

"Do you wish me to kiss you?" he asked quietly.

She would not lie. "Aye," she answered, low.

He shook his head slowly. "'Twould not serve either of us, milady."

"Speak only for yourself. It might serve me very well."

"Indeed, it might." His breathing had quickened. "Do you believe that I'm afraid of kissing you?"

"I believe you are afraid of love."

"Love makes men do strange things."

"From what I've seen, men do strange things no matter. Why not for love?"

He met her gaze steadily. "You are a fey temptress." His hand doubled into a fist and he pushed her chin gently with it. "Come along."

With that, he took her arm and turned her firmly toward the path leading back up to the horses. His destrier danced sideways when he approached. His large hands circled Arrah's waist and he lifted her effortlessly onto the back of her own white-maned horse.

"Did I ask a question that you could not answer?" she pressed. "Is that why you are moving me along like a hen shooing a chick?"

"'Tis not that I can't answer. 'Tis that I do not choose to answer," he replied, mounting his horse.

"'Tis no difference. You'll not muddle me with your words. Plain and simple, be honest enough to admit that you want to kiss me and are afraid to do so."

"I've no need to admit anything," he denied.

"Mayhap you are the sort of man who would kiss a maiden and try to take it back."

"Hah! And mayhap you'd be the sort of maiden who wouldn't *give* it back."

"Now who's the foolish one?"

"Not I. You can keep your magic lips to yourself."

A sudden, Arrah burst out in giggles at the nonsense passing between them. She laughed until her cheeks were glowing red.

"Am I your jester then?" He rolled his eyes.

"Stop . . . stop." She continued to laugh, clasping clumps of her horse's mane to keep her balance. "You'll have me falling off my horse." She brushed tears of mirth from the corners of her eyes. "We must talk of something else."

"Milady's choice."

Stillness followed while she settled her thoughts. "Can I ask you another question?"

"Aye, you have already."

"If you do not like the cold, why do you dwell here? Even in summer 'tis chilly," she said.

"The castle, the loch and the land are my birthright. A man does not leave his birthright. I spent my childhood here roaming alone. The loch and mountains are the finest garden in the five kingdoms for a child." His voice held a touch of wistfulness. "Even now it has its own special treasures and joys. I might lie upon my back watching the hawks hang in the blue until I sway below them like a riding ship. Or I might lie, chin over a cliff, and see the rabbits scattering and scuttling in the sun, or the fox, red-gold, slip past. Walking, I might surprise a stoat dancing all alone by himself. Aye, I was born here, and I'll die here."

Arrah was touched by the depth of his fealty to the land, and she was a little sad for the lonely boy who'd wandered wild. "My childhood in Myr was much the same, though I had many companions. Each day seemed all loveliness, all peace and happiness."

Where the path rose upward aromatic herbs nestled among the stones. She spied tiny leaves that smelled like incense, sage and thyme flowers, and golden gorse against the hillock. Mayhap, she thought, Myr did not hold all the wonders of the earth.

Voicing her comparisons, she said, "It does not snow in Myr, nor storm."

"Beway," he said, "have you never seen snow?"

"Nay."

"Nor storm?"

"Nay. Though the mists sometimes turn into a gentle rain."

"Och, you've not lived if you've not witnessed thunder upon the mountain or a gale whipping waves upon the loch."

In an attempt to better him, she returned, "And you've not lived until you've seen a hundred arching rainbows shining in the sky or the swan maidens dancing over the lake of glass, treading upon the reflection of stars."

"Mayhap, neither one of us have yet lived."

She looked over at him, and seeing the amused sparkle in his eyes she smiled, and he smiled. And she plainly knew that there was more meant in his words than said.

Side by side, they rode over the sloping hills. Arrah's spirit opened to the great expanse of sky above. She gazed around herself with delight, allowing her eyes to see the loch and mountains with a clarity of vision.

True, the landscape was far from friendly compared to Myr's. Here, earth's granite bones jutted up in rocky tors and lofty peaks. Here there were serpents that spat poison, thorns and thistles and predators that tore flesh apart. *Aye,* she thought, *here fear is alive—but so is love.*

Chapter

5

The sun was dropping below the hills when Arrah found Sib in the anteroom of the feast hall. Behind Sib, the hall was in darkness but for the skull wall sconces that glowed grotesquely against the coming night.

For a moment Arrah surveyed Sib from head to toe. A tunic of chain mail draped across her narrow shoulders and hung down past her knees. At her tiny waist was cinched, twice round, a scabbard sheathing a sword near as tall as Sib herself. A black-plumed helmet bedecked her head, covering hair that stuck out in a hopeless tangle. Upon her feet she wore boots that were spurred with heavy silver and that almost reached her hips.

Sib stuck out her hand. "Look at my leather gauntlets."

"Where did you find all this?"

Her eyes bright, she said, "Exploring. Do you think I look fine enough to make Camlan the Unsmiling smile?"

Arrah did not want to dash her hopes. Aye, he might smile, she thought, but not in the way Sib hoped. "Sib," she began gently, "you want a man who loves you for yourself, not for your outward appearances."

In that moment the Fianna entered the hall. Before Arrah could stop her, Sib turned and, with encumbered steps, intersected Camlan's path.

With both hands gripping the hilt, she drew her sword from the scabbard and announced, "I pledge my fealty to Camlan the Unsmiling."

Camlan rounded on her. "What costume is this? 'Tis out of fashion. Did you collide with a tinker's cart?" He drew his own sword amid the hearty laughter of the other men, and not ungently swatted her upon the rump with the sword's flat side. "I dub you bumpkin, buffoon and booka. Be off with you."

Sib stood stunned, her lower lip quivering. The sword dropped from her hand with a metallic ring that quieted the laughter.

Her own stomach sinking, Arrah looked past Camlan and to Traeth, who like herself stood a witness to the sad encounter.

They looked at each other, and then Traeth strode toward her and offered his arm. "Come sit at my side and eat."

Arrah was torn.

Traeth knew, and said, "Let her be. You cannot take her pain upon yourself. She must learn her own hard lessons."

Arrah frowned with resignation and placed her hand upon his arm. He led her to a spot amid the assemblage of warriors, who were now eating and drinking their fill at the long wooden tables.

She reached for a green apple, not seeing anything more palatable amid the trenchers of roasted game. "Your warriors seemed very excited this evening."

"We will be riding out tonight," he said lightly.

"And what will you do?"

"What we do best—slay dragons and rescue lovely maidens."

She gave him a blank look. "But I thought dragons were a rarity in the five kingdoms, and you said you had no use for women."

He smiled, unable to chew and speak at the same time. Arrah waited for him to answer. At last he said, "In truth we are out for a night of adventure. Word has come that halflings are trespassing in the borderlands."

"Halflings?" questioned Arrah.

"They are the cross spawn of Sidhe and the realm of men. They dwell in the haunted borderlands, making mischief and worse. You remember the luminous orb I showed you in the tower chamber?"

She nodded her head. "Aye."

"The halflings desire such treasures like the orb to bring light to their dark world of the in-between."

"Beway," she breathed, intrigued.

"The orbs are very rare and spawn only in one cave on the edge of the loch. The halflings have attempted to raid us before, leaving devastation in their wake. 'Tis my duty as mage to protect all in my domain."

"Will that be your errand this night?"

"Aye. Would you like to ride with us?"

"Nay. I'm content here."

"So, you have no sense of adventure after all." He took a sip from a golden goblet.

"I have a fair sense of self-preservation," she returned.

"That is a dull affair, milady."

"We cannot all be dragon slayers, you know. And besides, I do not think it so much a matter of slaying dragons as embracing them."

"I have never thought of that."

"I'll bet not," she returned.

"You've no need to be sarcastic," he said, rising to his feet. "Come along and we'll commence your first adventure."

Her lips framed a refusal, but no words came. She looked at him, suddenly aware that her resistance to adventure was quickly departing.

He gave a short command. His Fianna needed no second urging. They came to their feet, their polished armor gleaming in the hearth light.

Between one moment and the next she found herself mounted on the same white destrier. For some reason the horse seemed much taller and the ground much farther away. The drawbridge stretched before her, a yawning portal to adventure.

Around her the Fianna gathered themselves, mounting and reining back their restless steeds. They appeared neither boisterous nor grim, merely alert and on their mark for the event ahead.

Arrah wondered what that event might be as they clattered across the drawbridge, thirty strong or more. The rising moonlight shone softly on the horses' flanks, on silver scabbard and iron mail.

Traeth led them above the loch and up a forest track. The track was uneven and strewn with sharp boulders, and the mountain shadows expanded to become squat monsters shouldering the night. Game scattered at the sound and sight of such a riding force.

Traeth dropped back by her side. "If you are to ride with my Fianna, you must ride proud. Straighten your shoulders, milady, and look as if you've no fear of anything on earth."

"Do I look frightened?" she asked, suddenly aware that her features were tensed into an unseemly grimace.

"Go slowly, and use your horse's mouth gently. You'd not wish him to bolt and throw you at the sight of our first dragon."

"And what sort of dragon will that be?" she asked.

She knew there were all kinds—swamp dragons, river dragons, forest dragons . . .

"The two-legged sort, milady."

She did as he bid, tightening the reins with great care. Her horse fell back as Fergus Dry Lips took her place beside Traeth.

The ranks of the Fianna opened around her and then closed again. In a matter of seconds she was protected on every side by men whose most precious virtue seemed to be their ability to tower in their saddles like the legendary gods of old earth.

They rode onward into the cool gloaming of evening, through stands of ancient fir and fragile green birch, over darkening hills. And in all that quiet world of forest, sky and mountain there was no sound but the wind and the clattering of hooves, and the creak and jangle of leather and bit. On they went, each one occupied with his own thoughts, silent and withdrawn.

The pace slowed perceptibly, and she saw Traeth's hand raise, signaling a halt. A dozen men left the group and turned their horses south. Then around her the others dismounted. Dath Bright Spear, who was closest, gave Arrah a steadying hand as she slipped to the ground; and she had need of that support. Her legs stiff as straw, she staggered to a boulder and eased herself down.

After he had spoken in a low voice to the men, Traeth came to sit beside her and shared a cool draught of mead from a slender leather flask.

"Are we near your two-legged dragon?" she whispered.

"Not so near that you must whisper," he said, amused. "How do you feel?"

She returned the flask to him, then looked before her at the mountains lifting one behind the other, and the towering treetops disappearing into the blue night sky. "Good."

She spied a new star above a gorge. It hung like a lantern, lighting the dark vastness lying quietly below. "You see that star to the east?" she asked, raising her forefinger.

"Aye," he said.

"I feel like I would like to touch it. Have you ever wanted to touch a star?"

"Mayhap when I was a child, but not recently," he said.

"All of us, whether man or swan maiden, come from the stars. Each of us has our own quality of light, a light that can be soft as a candle or bright as the sun. In coming together in shared love, we can weave the warp and weft of the universe back together again and return home to the stars."

He gave a half-smile. "'Tis a grand notion, milady, and I wish you good fortune in your return to the stars, but I'm content to keep my feet flat upon the earth." He stood up and stretched, and pulled her up beside himself. "Now begins the adventure. You must stay where I leave you, no matter what happens."

She frowned. "What sort of adventure is that?"

"The sort that ends well," he said, putting his hands on her waist and guiding her to her horse.

All about her the Fianna swung up into their saddles, more than eager.

Arrah found it exceedingly painful to mount her horse again so soon, but she lifted her chin and contained any sigh or groan that might give her away.

They began to move, slowly and with great care. She wanted to ask Traeth why he had brought her along if he only intended to leave her. But she thought better of it.

Suddenly, the Fianna halted. They waited, it seemed to her, an interminable length of time. Traeth sat upon his horse, one arm resting across the pommel. Arrah did not take her eyes off him. His face was impassive and self-assured, yet there was a hint of latent violence about him. It was subtle, but frightening to contemplate.

In that moment she knew him, and the riddle of man as well.

It was as he had said: In each man lived two men—one who could smile with a deep and honest warmth, and another, cold and ruthless, and so implacable that mercy was surely unknown to him.

He shifted to alertness. She could hear nothing, but caught a whiff of a most unpleasant odor. On either side of her the men lowered their hands upon their sword hilts. One of the Fianna reached for her bridle and held her horse back as the others moved forward.

Traeth turned to her. "Keep heart, milady," he said softly, giving her the incredible white flash of his smile.

Then, letting loose her bridle, the last man left, silently, men and horses disappearing among the trees like specters. There was no sound at all, only the fetid odor that she soon realized was the odor of death. Could she alone smell it? Were they riding to their deaths?

She waited, there in the dark where nothing stirred but the sighing wind. She waited for a sign or sound, a cry, a clash of steel. All the while, she was caught in a spell of anticipation.

The cry came first, shrill and far away. Then a great shouting arose and the metallic clatter of swords carried on the night air too clearly. Though she held tight to the reins, her horse reared its forelegs to the sky and came near to throwing her off.

The horse dropped, danced sideways, tossed its mane wildly and with a snort leaped forward. Arrah was too startled to do more than try to keep her balance on the charging war-horse. A birch limb slapped her face with a stinging blow. The horse topped a rise and galloped straight into the fray of confusion and chaos.

Suddenly surrounded by the surging, shapeless mass of battle, the horse stopped dead. Arrah flew over the horse's head to land on the ground with a resounding thud that shook her nearly senseless. Following her instincts as blindly as the battle-excited horse had, she stood up unsteadily to ascertain if all her bones were still knit together. In the dim moonlight, amid shouts and screams and the glitter of swords, she looked for a place of safety. There wasn't one.

Before her Arrah faced a chariot that was a masterpiece of elven art. Carved into the silvered wood were countless tiny pictures and glyphs that writhed and shivered with every movement of the chariot. A dark covering banded the wheels, and set in the hubs were fitted knives. Inside was a short, hairless dwarf whose skin was bone-white, giving his head a skull-like appearance. Beside him stood a halfling. He held the reins of a great, snorting catoblepas with great care as his master wielded a long sword.

Then, standing alone and dumbstruck in the midst of the strife, she saw the chariot coming toward her. The dwarf, with a fierce yell swelling his throat and a bare sword in his grip, lunged at her.

She saw clearly that he meant to run her through with that sword. Never had she seen the look of stark hatred in someone's face, or eyes so flat and lifeless. He fully meant to kill her.

All fear left her; there was only pure astonishment that such mindless acts could happen. She stared at the wicked point of the sword with no hope of escape. She wanted to weep with frantic disappointment.

But she did not die. She instinctively took a backward step, and the sword tip grazed her shoulder. But he did not follow through with another attack to her heart, for suddenly a long sword materialized as if out of thin air. The sword struck so powerful a blow that the dwarf's sword flew from his hand in a complete circle and, before Arrah's incredulous eyes, dropped to the ground. The dwarf's face stiffened into endless lines of surprise.

Then, looming above her, she saw the black gauntlet holding the sword hilt, and Traeth astride a horse. The horse's warm nostrils brushed across her face as she was swept up into the saddle by an arm that encircled her like a band of steel.

Shocked by the brutality of it all, she dared not move, and kept her face hidden against Traeth's leathers. She heard him shout, felt his horse break forward into a hard gallop and the thunder of horses shake the earth behind her.

After a time she became aware of a sticky wetness on her upper arm. She was bleeding from the small wound.

When they had ridden for what seemed like half the night, Traeth reined in his horse and she lifted her head at last to face him. He looked past her and to his men behind.

Dath Bright Spear rode up to his side.

"How do we fare?" Traeth asked briskly.

"We're all of a piece," said Bright Spear. "But we lost her horse."

"'Twill end up meat for the halflings, but it can't be helped," he said.

Arrah felt a great pang of remorse for so fine an animal to come to such an end.

"Have the Fianna remain here until morning. I doubt if they will follow us to Rhune Castle, but we best keep guard. I'll take the woman and go ahead."

He rode over the hill and down into a glen, wooded along the banks of the loch. The starlight touched the trees and water with gilded silver, and the shadows were velvet-soft and black. There was no wind there, only the quiet night and the sweet fragrances of bell heather.

He dismounted without a word and lifted Arrah from his destrier. Feeling giddy, she was grateful for the strong support of his hand, but she would have gladly exchanged it for an assuring word that the adventure was over.

"Sit down, Arrah of Myr," he said. Then, he took off the bridle and saddle, and the horse nuzzled a tuft of grass.

Obeying him, she sat on the mossy bank. The heavy dew was cool and wet beneath her. Returning to her side, he knelt on one leg and examined her shoulder in the dim light.

He began to ease her tunic off.

She stared at him, but did not protest. His eyes were black and shadowed as they met hers. "I must see your wound," he said. She stifled a gasp as the dried blood and cloth pulled away, leaving her upper body exposed.

"'Tis a clean cut," he enlightened. "Not much more than a scratch. You must have caught only the sword tip as he lunged."

"I'm sorry to have lost the horse," she began hesitantly.

He might not have heard her, for all the attention he paid her apology. She watched his large hands move carefully over the white skin of her arm.

"The wound must be washed," he said. "And I need to cleanse myself of the war fire as well. Take off your clothes and come down to the water."

"'Tis very cold," she challenged, knowing he did not like the cold.

"Do not worry on my account. The rush of it renews me."

Puzzling, she stood and slipped out of her leggings.

She wondered if all the Fianna followed such a ritual after a battle.

He stripped down quickly. This time he did not hesitate but jumped into the water with vigorous abandonment. He submerged and then burst out of the shattering obsidian surface with a hearty shout.

She followed, breaking into a cry of exaltation. Hair flying, arms spread into wings, she hurled herself into the loch. The icy water bit her face as she skidded across its glassy mirror. Deeper and deeper into the chilling, numbing darkness she went; then she came up for breath. She gasped for sweet air and, turning on her back, floated.

She felt a familiar freedom as the water caressed her bare skin, and she gazed up at the stars. Her body tingled with the delight of life.

Traeth surfaced, his face within inches of her own. The wet spray of his released breath sprinkled her cheek. Masculine, dangerous and familiar, his face held clean-lined composure. His eyes widened slightly, and moonlight speared the dark filaments of his irises. The nostrils of his sovereign nose flared for more breath while his cavalier lips parted victoriously.

Terwen had said that to men freedom meant the right to go to war. Arrah wondered a moment and then asked him, "What is war?"

His eyes flickered over her for no more than a brief instant before he answered. "War is the taking of what is not offered."

She asked another question. "What is the opposite of war?"

His eyes narrowed circumspectly, and then he returned, "Giving."

"I do not agree," she said.

"You do not?" His dark brow lifted.

"No, I do not. Must I always agree with you?"

He shrugged. "I suppose not. So, what do you believe is the opposite of war?"

"Receiving what is offered," she said.

He ruminated on the idea and then said, "Mayhap."

"If you could receive what is offered, you would not have to go to war." It was all becoming very clear to Arrah, the differences between men and women and between the realms of Myr and men. As a swan maiden, her innate gift to all was the gift of love. Men had not yet mastered the ability to receive love, and more often feared an open heart. Hence, whenever a swan maiden offered her gift, the man became hopelessly enchanted because of his inability to open himself to that essence. She thought of Sib and Camlan the Unsmiling. He could not receive her love because he only knew how to take what was not offered.

"Aye," Traeth continued, "but what if nothing is offered?"

"'Tis easy," she said lightly. "You must then offer something yourself."

"'Tis good advice." His face lost all flippancy.

He caught her hair and wound it around his fist, pulling her to him. His face hovered close to hers—so close that she saw desire in the softening of his jaw and the glowing threads of fire in the dark pools of his eyes.

Arrah breathed deeply. Her whole body tingled like faerie chimes at dawn. Between them, the air vibrated. Would he kiss her lips? Would he risk enchantment?

One of his hands supported the small of her back while the other cradled and lifted her hips so that she floated beside him. He smoothed her skin, running his hands down her hips onto her thighs, avoiding the center of her belly, and her mound.

Under his touch, she thought her bones would dissolve.

Softly smoothing, as if her skin were satin, he bestowed continuous caresses with the palm of his hand over her shoulders, following the full swell of her breasts down to the soft flesh of her belly, where the water lapped and pooled. His strokes, layered one on the other, moved with the ebbing and flowing currents of water.

With the lightest brushing of his fingertips, he circled the soft indentation of her stomach, moving down to the nest of her womanhood. His touch pleasured her. He aroused her in ways she'd never imagined, even in dreaming moments. He pressed gently with the heel of his hand on her woman's mound.

Fire shot through Arrah. On the watery bed, she arched to the pressure of his palm as she felt the strengthening support of his hand on the small of her back. Under his preening, she felt more woman than swan.

Tenderly, she reached her hands out, cupped his dark head and drew his face down to hers.

"Kiss me," she urged, her voice low.

His arms encircled her. He pulled her upright from the water and held her close to him. She was acutely aware of his manhood, hard against the soft hollow of her belly. Her palms relaxed against his chest, and then her hands slid beneath his arms to curl around his back.

"Nay, milady. I'll not kiss you," he said with dogged restraint.

"But 'tis offered. Receive me," she said with a rare depth of sincerity. She smelled his body, male and musk, and she smelled her own wantonness. Pressed against his muscled chest, her nipples began to tingle, and his rigid rod burned like a spear's point on her skin. His one hand let loose her hair and slid down across the slickness of her hips.

More boldly, she crossed boundaries and let her hands track down the warm heat of his muscled torso to his hard buttocks. Her eyes searched the black-fired depths of his. He nuzzled her cheek, carefully avoiding her lips.

A low hum of pleasure trembled in his throat, and he shifted his hips to better mold himself to the juncture of hers. A giant yearning flamed within Arrah, more powerful than she could fight. Her lips were at his throat, then his chest. When her tongue circled his dark nipples, he moaned with pleasure.

Her senses gyrated around and around. A secret clarity began opening within her like dancing light. In this bliss she held him, held everything alive—earth, sea and fire. She was alive. She ached—for him.

"I'm opening to you. . . . Receive me," she rasped as if she were dying.

She heard his indrawn breath and felt his hand gather her hair and pull her head back to face his own. She raised her searching gaze to his. His eyes flashed the color of the night and scalded her with their intensity.

Reluctantly, she drew back. She knew he could not receive her. He was a warrior and could take only what was not offered.

She felt his measured appraisal. "Fold your wings, milady. I'll not fall under your enchantments this night or any other." His hands on her waist, he gently guided her from the water and up the embankment.

Arrah could not speak. Her body was near to collapsing from disappointment and frustration. He had teased her, captured and seduced her from the beginning. He called her to him, then pushed her away. She did not understand the way of love in the world of men. Mayhap there was no love in him at all.

Traeth released a tense breath as he followed Arrah

up the lochshore. Though in outward appearance he was in control, inwardly a battle was raging. He was acutely conscious of her femininity and his desire for her. Watching her grace and beauty fired within him feelings he'd fervently wished to suppress. He had no wish to suffer the fate of his father and fall victim to the sickness of love's enchantment that had eventually led the hapless man to a languishing death. A voice counseled him to return her swan skin and send her back to Myr. Yet, the greater part of him resisted . . . the part of him that wanted her.

Aye, he chastised himself. *I need no kiss to become bewitched. I'm already a fool without it.*

After they dressed, he spread his cloak on the ground for her comfort and then built a campfire. She sat close, drying her damp hair in the fire's warmth.

He knelt down beside her. "How is your shoulder?"

"Not painful. I will heal."

"You should have obeyed me and stayed where I left you."

"I did not disobey intentionally. I could not hold the destrier back from the battle."

"Aye, maybe 'twas my error in giving you a seasoned war-horse. And what did you think of your first battle?" he asked. He leaned his weight on one arm while the other rested casually across his knee. "Were you frightened?"

"Aye, 'tis frightening to face the point of a sword and realize the man behind it means to kill you."

"What were you thinking," he asked quietly, "in the last moment before he lunged at you?"

"I thought 'twas so foolish to kill someone you did not know."

He smiled. "Do you think it easier to kill someone you know?"

"Nay, I think it would be harder. I did discover something, though." She rubbed her chin thoughtfully.

"What was that?"

"I discovered that fear is excitement without breath. As I stood frozen, I could not move a muscle. Then, I began to breathe and the fear left. I saw no fear in the faces of the Fianna. In truth, I wish I had."

"Why?"

She lowered her eyes. "I saw no feeling at all in their faces."

"Look at me, Arrah."

She lifted her gaze. Her innocence disarmed him, but he continued. "One does not need feelings to kill. Without remorse, I have killed many men, and doubtless will kill many more before one returns the favor."

She seemed to wince at his callousness.

He tossed a twig into the fire and said, "I have told you the truth, and if the truth does not please you, 'tis your own kettle to stir."

He looked at her small hands clasped delicately in the cleft of her lap, her long hair flowing down over her shoulders, and her strange, ever-changing eyes glowing as softly as a candlewick. She knew nothing of life.

He waited for her to speak, but somehow he knew she would say nothing more. In some ways she understood him far too well, and the words left unsaid were as clear to him as those spoken.

Then, she smiled at him, a smile that left him shaken and entranced, and wanting the feel of those soft, smiling lips upon his.

He shifted, saying, "We should sleep before the dawn comes."

"Here?" she asked uncertainly.

"Here," he returned decisively. "Unless you've a complaint about using me as a feather pillow."

He moved beside her, and slipped one arm beneath her to hold her close against him. Her head rested on his leathers.

"Can you hear my heart beat?" he asked.

"Aye," she answered.

"Then there's your proof that I'm not so heartless a man as you believe."

"I have never said you had no heart. 'Tis your inability to listen to it that's the misfortune."

He chuckled and settled back. "The stars are close tonight," he said quietly.

"Close enough to touch if one wished to."

"And do you wish to?"

"You know I always wish to," she answered drowsily, and then yawned.

"Soon you'll be dreaming of plucking stars."

"Do you dream?" she asked.

"All men dream, else life would ofttimes be unendurable."

"What do you dream?"

"I don't always remember my dreams. As a child I could bring my dreams back."

"What do you mean?"

"'Twas a pastime for me. I was lonely and for want of playmates I would call upon the images in my dreams. They kept me safe—safe from want, from fear and loneliness. Unfortunately, because they were illusions, by the end of the day they faded out of sight." He laughed a little.

"That is a wonderful gift to create your dreams, if only for a day."

"As a boy, I fashioned a very pleasant vision of myself as a sorcerer of no mean cunning."

"And now 'tis true. You are the Mage of the Dragon's Mouth."

"Aye, I'm a weather-worker, a master of the elements. In battle I can call in wind, hail and thunder to scatter the enemy. I know how to bind and loose the winds, and how to conjure rain or roaring flame. I can bring down pestilence and drought, famine and frost."

"For what end do you do this?"

"For no end at all. You are truly innocent of life," he said easily.

"But could you not as well bring sun and rain to the farmer's field and wind to the sails of the mariner?"

"And return every fallen fledgling to its nest and rescue each flagging fawn from the stalking predator?" he added dryly. "Nay, sweet Arrah, I cannot. 'Tis not my dream to be so gallant. I'm a warrior of the Fianna."

After a brief silence she said, "I've heard it said that starlight casts a spell on any who sleep under it. Mayhap you'll dream a new dream for yourself."

He smiled to himself, thinking she was not unlike most women. "I do not wish to dream a new dream for myself. I'm content to be who I am. There is a saying, 'When a man looks upon a maid he sees something ethereal. When a maid looks upon a man, she sees a piece of material.' You'll not change the fabric of who I am, my peaceful swan heart."

She lowered her finely shadowed lids. He had not meant to offend her. His eyes traveled over her face, marveling at the golden lashes lowered against the white alabaster cheekbones, the perfect nose whose polished nub begged for kissing, the sensual curve of her mouth and the pleasure it promised.

The more he looked, the more he realized that if he were under enchantment's spell he would do anything for her. It was within his capacity to change the terrain of the land, create lakes where there were none, level forests into plains. And amid such great feats he might even consider changing the terrain of his own heart and soul to please her.

Aye, she was dangerous, more dangerous than any warlord, wizard or sorcerer he'd ever encountered.

Chapter

Go on, go on," Arrah said encouragingly. Sib was on her knees before a door latch in the tower of the dragon's claw.

Sib's nostrils tightened with a deep intake of breath. She exhaled through her mouth and Arrah heard the releasing click of lock.

"Is this the last?" asked Sib hopefully.

"No. I plan to search every room and tower, every nook and cranny in this castle for my swan skin. And you must help me."

"'Twill be hopeless," whined Sib. "The castle has three towers and at least a hundred doors each. The halls change and the rooms disappear. 'Tis haunted by weird and terrifying monstrosities. We'll be found babbling gibberish and our hair turned white to the roots."

"No matter," Arrah said as Sib came to her feet and opened the door. "What else is there to do in this lonely place now the Fianna are off chasing their enemies?"

"I wish I were with them," declared Sib.

"So, your fair Camlan refused to take you along?"

"He did," pouted Sib. "But I've another scheme where he's concerned."

"What is that?"

"I'm keeping my own counsel, dear sister," she snipped.

Arrah sighed with relief. That meant she had no scheme at all. Sib ever relied on spontaneity. "Let us see what this room holds," she said, unthwarted.

It was close to evening when the Fianna returned to Rhune Castle. Traeth walked slowly through the upper levels, entering each door in turn or calling Arrah's name through the corridors. A heavy foreboding nestled in his thoughts. What if she had found her swan skin through some form of divination? What if she'd escaped?

Traeth felt a sinking in the pit of his stomach. He stood in an empty chamber before a cold hearth, overcome by a feeling of abandonment. 'Twas an old emptiness. . . . He was a small boy again playing beside his mother near the loch when a dark-cloaked man appeared, speaking to his mother in words he could not understand. The man struck her with a hazel wand and she was transformed into a white deer. With a longing glance from the brown sloe eyes, the deer looked at him, then followed the dark man up the mountain. After crying for a time, he fell asleep, and when he awoke Carne the Aged stood over him, smiling kindly. He had never learned what happened to his mother, but it was sorcery, to be sure.

Returning to the hall, Traeth sent some of the Fianna to search for Arrah through the castle and around the loch.

Camlan the Unsmiling grumbled at what in his opinion was a waste of time. He did not hesitate to air his relief at not having his familiar shadow tagging along after him. "If the pair have left, 'tis good riddance, I say."

Surprisingly, Traeth rounded on him and snapped, "Your manners leave much to be desired. Take care, lest I teach you some."

Camlan looked uncomfortable. For a few moments the hall was so quiet they could hear the flames eating away at the dried wood.

"If my words offended you, then I apologize," Camlan said. "I meant to cast no slur upon the lady's honor."

Traeth's eyes circled the faces of his Fianna. "If any man passes insult upon the lady Arrah of Myr, it will be taken as an insult to me."

Dath Bright Spear stepped forward. "You shame us to suppose that we would insult the lady." He placed a hand upon the hilt of his sword. "I swear by my sword to protect the lady Arrah of Myr from all harm."

Traeth had always taken pride in his justice, and had sought to be fair. "I accept your oath of fealty, Bright Spear."

The others murmured support as well and the air cleared somewhat. Traeth left the hall making the inward vow that if he found Arrah of Myr, he'd not lose her again.

For the whole of the afternoon and into late night, Arrah diligently nudged Sib through the highs and lows of Rhune Castle. Sib crept from door to door, having an immensely good time releasing each lock and throwing open each door. Behind one was the armory, behind another the kitchens. All manner of holdings were behind the doors and Sib chortled with delight at every wonderful and exotic discovery.

Around midnight, they met the end of a corridor, and a blank wall.

"I've enough of searching," Sib declared. "Besides, this is the last candle, and it's near spent."

"Wait," said Arrah in a subdued voice. Suddenly, a door appeared where there was no door before.

Despite her uneasiness, Arrah said, "Surely, we can't pass it by."

"I can pass it by," sighed Sib. "My feet hurt and I'm hungry."

As if she were on her last gasp, Sib puffed one small breath into the lock eye. The door not only clicked, but swung open without aid.

It was so dark inside they could not see.

A cold chill tingled down Arrah's back. She smelled death. "I'll go first," said Arrah, stooping through the doorway.

"What makes you so brave?" challenged Sib, remaining rooted where she was.

"I want my swan skin."

"I don't feel good about this," said Sib. Then she succumbed to her own natural curiosity, and stepped after Arrah into the chamber.

It was empty—completely, absolutely empty. No windows, no hearth, no furniture.

"'Tis a great waste of time," said Sib, turning back.

"No, wait!" commanded Arrah. "Look, there is a trapdoor right in the middle of the floor." She walked over and reached down for the iron ring pull. "I can't manage it myself; come help me."

Reluctantly, Sib went to her side and slipped her slim fingers into the ring pull. "Pull," she groaned. At the same moment the door gave way and she accidentally dropped the candle down the yawning black opening.

Both screamed at once, for in the light they saw a mire of blackened bones and skulls stacked like a pyramid of apples.

They dropped the trapdoor, then fell against each other gasping, their chests heaving.

"We've found the heart of evil!" cried Sib.

"I fear 'tis so. Run!" Arrah shoved Sib forward as

both scrambled out of the chamber. All was black, but it made no difference in their headlong race through the twists and turns of the castle's bowels.

Arrah heard the clomp of boots. Her heart was pounding at a rabbit's pace, and at first she thought the sounds came from behind, as if the bones themselves were in hot pursuit.

Suddenly, she was blinded by torchlight.

"Who's there?" a deep voice roared.

Strong arms caught her in an unrelenting grip. Terror filled her, but she was helpless against that strength.

"Let me free!" she cried, struggling in the hard clamp of those arms.

"By the dragon's blood!" the voice swore. "'Tis I, Traeth of Rhune."

Her thrashing tumbled them both to the stone floor. Then she opened her eyes and saw his face within inches of her own, and all her resistance left.

"'Tis you," she said, her pulse slowing.

"Who did you think it was?"

"The bones."

"'The bones'?" he echoed. Then, he started to laugh. Another, and then another, voice joined in the mirth.

She looked up and saw Carne the Aged and Bright Spear. Sib was leaning against the wall, catching her breath.

"So you've snooped yourself right into the catacombs of the castle. No wonder you're struck with fright," said Carne the Aged.

Traeth gently untangled himself and came to his feet, lifting her with him.

She felt foolish and dared not look at him.

"We returned early evening. When I could not find you I assumed you had fled . . . or were lost in the castle. We've been searching for you for hours," Traeth said. "Now, you are found and safe." He enclosed Arrah in the protective circle of one arm. "Come ahead. I've a surprise for you."

He had her full attention now.

Within minutes they were in the feast hall. Arrah felt great relief at seeing the flaming warmth of the twin dragon hearths. Sib darted to sit at the feet of Camlan the Unsmiling. He ignored her, but she remained undaunted.

"Come here, milady. I've something to show you," invited Traeth.

She turned to see him undoing the heavy leather straps encircling a chest, not unlike the one that he had placed her swan skin in. Hoped leaped in her heart. Was her swan skin inside? Would he return it?

"'Tis not more bones is it?" Sib mumbled.

Traeth smiled and shook his head. "Nay, 'tis treasure from the five kingdoms," he said, teasing everyone by taking his time with the straps. "Gems and gold, and a few puddings stolen from a king's table."

"If this treasure is ill-got, I want none of it," announced Arrah, resting her hands upon her hips.

He threw back the carved lid, and she drew a long, unsteady breath and dropped her hands to her sides. The firelight caressed rich and satiny fabrics in a gay profusion of colors. Crimsons and tawny golds, greens with the deep fire of emeralds, magentas and palest blues whirled before her wide eyes. It was better than her daydreams.

"May I touch them?" she asked politely, but reached inside before he answered.

She pulled out gowns one by one. The first was of spun gold like dew in morning sunlight; another was a delicate blue encrusted with sea pearls and boasting petticoats sprinkled with flowers, much like a spring meadow after rain.

The last, a dragonfly silk, elegant and glowing with changing colors, she held to her cheek in wordless wonder. Its softness was like the skin of a wee babe or the downy underside of a feathered breast. It reminded her of a snowflake alighting on the tip of her tongue, the first stirring of a summer breeze and the pale green tree moss in the deepest woods, all in one.

"Choose," said Traeth. "Which pleases you the most?"

She looked up at him, leaning over her, his eyes steady on her face, and she suddenly blushed. She'd forgotten herself completely.

"What is it?" he asked with a hint of surprise in his face.

"I've never experienced the joy of possessing," she confessed. "Whatever would I do with such as this?"

He laughed at her. Reaching for her hand, he pulled her up. "Wear it."

She was much too enchanted with the gown to decline.

"I want to see myself," she said.

A brief request to Bright Spear, and Traeth soon saw that a tall freestanding looking glass was placed before Arrah. Using it as screen of privacy, she slipped from her leggings and tunic and into the gown. Its softness felt wonderful upon her bare skin. The front scooped low and the silk cascaded down over the swell of her hips to the floor.

In a magical whisper of silk, she twirled around and took glee at being able to see herself from all angles. The boisterous gathering of warriors seemed to fade away and she stood alone, wholly bewitched by her own reflection.

At the sight of her, Carne the Aged said with geniality, "By heath and heaven, ye're enough to awaken the mischief in an old sorcerer."

She whirled before him. "'Tis my own mischief that awakens from its beauty."

"And mine as well," Traeth said from behind her.

She turned hastily, and her gown brushed against his boots. His dark eyes scanned her carelessly, as if his thoughts were only of her and the way she looked to him at that moment.

He offered his hand, "Come away. We should have a walk in the moonlight."

After a brief glance at Sib, who stood nearby, Arrah accepted. She saw envy in Sib's face and knew that she ached to wear such a gown as well. She wanted to find a way to tell Sib that her time was coming, but knew that she would not be convinced. Arrah cast an eye to Camlan the Unsmiling, who sat, with back turned, not far from Sib. He might come to rue the day he snubbed her, Arrah thought.

It was a glorious night outside, pleasantly warm without wind. Blossoming growth scented the air about her with a haunting sweetness.

Traeth's hand was under her arm, leading her across the courtyard and through a doorway in the battlement wall, then steadying her down steep stairs to a narrow path winding among boulders to the loch's edge. A curragh was moored on the water.

"Climb in," said Traeth, "I'll take you on a moonlight ride."

He lifted her across the intervening space and deposited her firmly inside. She watched him bend his back to the oars with an easy regularity of pace that rippled the muscles in his shoulders. While they moved over the still surface of the water, she first heard the thin thread of sound coming unexpectedly out of the night.

The soft strains seemed so close to her, almost within the curragh, that she looked around for a harper plucking his strings. But despite her clear view in all directions, she could see no one but Traeth, and his hands were on the oars. The eerie melody continued, and so did the eerie feeling.

"Faerie music, the music that lures travelers out of this world," he said. "Do you hear it?"

"Aye, I hear," she returned. "I have heard this music before, the night you captured me. I thought it came from Rhune Castle."

"Nay, there is no harper at Rhune Castle."

The waves lapped against the sides of the curragh as Traeth rowed. At last they reached the tip of a headland, a desolate wilderness of rock and cliffs worn smooth by centuries of loch storms.

Her gown caught on the edge of the curragh, and he caught her in his arms. "I should have worn my leggings. They'd be better suited for exploring."

"But not nearly so enticing," he said, then without ceremony lifted her onto the shore and secured the curragh.

The rising moon provided enough light as he led her up a winding path lined by blackened boulders. "Have you ever heard of a dragon's hoard?"

She shook her head, too intrigued to speak.

"All dragons have a hoard. 'Tis treasure the dragon protects." He slowed before a gaping hole surrounded by more ash-blackened stones.

Peering cautiously in, she saw a dark, downward-sloping passage. "Are you taking me inside?"

"Aye. Don't you want to go?"

"Are you sure there is no dragon in there?"

"I'm sure. 'Tis older than the loch itself, and no dragon has abided here for that long and more."

"Aye, I'll go."

She took his hand and entered the mouth of the cave. Keeping one hand in his and the other against the clammy wall, she inched forward. As they descended, the air became close and began to smell odd. Soon she identified the odor. Dragon—the cave smelled of dragon. Though the stink of a dragon's lair was legendary, the smell here did not stink, nor was it foul to her. Clearly, this cave had been inhabited by a fastidious loch dragon whose primal element was water. At length, the passage made a turn, and Traeth stopped.

The shadows were long and dark. The harp music seemed to encircle them now. Outside the air had been clean and sweet-smelling, but now she breathed the overpowering scents of ash, earth, moss and ancient dragon.

"Stay here," Traeth said, releasing her hand. She felt a little panic, standing in the unfamiliar space. Then, the darkness lifted. Traeth held in his hand a luminous sphere like the one she'd seen at Rhune Castle. Looking about, she saw others of different sizes attached to the walls amidst crimson lichen and exotic underground foliage. After another second of adjustment, Arrah's vision took full view of her surroundings.

It was a treasure chamber. Strewn all around were flashing piles of gold and gems, chests overflowing with pearls and exquisitely crafted jewelry, silver swords with gilded and bejeweled hilts, and other valuables beyond imagining. What caught her eye most was a shimmering pool in the cave's heart. At the foot of its trickling waterfall sat a harp. As the water cascaded down, its wet spray sprinkled over the harp strings, creating the music she had heard.

She turned to Traeth and said, "'Tis a magic harp."

"Aye, that and more," he agreed, putting aside the luminous orb. "'Tis the legendary Lyre of *Guivre.*"

Her mouth dropped open with surprise. "Even in Myr we've heard of the Lyre of *Guivre.* Its song is believed to heal all wounds and call back the spirit of the dying."

"And," he added, "just hearing its melody can bind forever the hearts of lovers."

She looked at him and smiled, then felt the smile

grow tremulous and unsure. "Do you believe that is happening to us now?" she asked.

"I don't know."

"Do you wish it?" she asked.

"No more than I wish to be enslaved by the enchantment of your kiss."

"Then why do you not return to me my swan skin?"

"When one walks along the edge of a precipice," he said, "there is often a great temptation to see how close one may venture to the brink without falling."

"You are edge-walking, then."

"Aye."

"I wish . . ." she began, and then stopped, drawing an unsteady breath.

His face was circumspect. "You wish what? Say it out."

"I wish that there were no magicks, no enchantments or spells. I wish that we could be but a man and woman, loving plain and simple."

"But neither of us are plain and simple. You are a swan maiden from Myr and I am the Mage of the Dragon's Mouth, and the moment we kiss will be far more dangerous than walking the edge of a cliff."

They looked at each other, and the world grew still and hushed. Neither heard the trickle of water or the lilting melody of the Lyre of *Guivre*. It was as if all other life had ceased to be for that one span of time, which belonged to them alone.

He was so close to her that his wide shoulders shut out the rest of the cave. She could see the small, steady pulse in his throat, and so she fastened her eyes on it and would not raise them to be further unsettled by his unswerving gaze, his mouth, the heavy fringe of black lashes shadowing his eyes.

"I think 'tis too late to pull back to safety, Arrah of Myr, and we shall know the meaning of disaster after all."

"Will it surely be disaster?"

"Aye," he said, his voice low and resigned. " 'Tis the nature of a cruel world."

She felt uncertain and shaken, the more so because she did not understand him fully. "We should go back," she said.

His hand touched her chin firmly, lifting her face to his. "We've long since lost any chance to turn back, Arrah. You have wanted my kiss; now you shall have it."

"You are under the spell of the Lyre of *Guivre,*" she said.

"Mayhap. But I have wanted you from the first," he confessed.

"Be patient," she hedged.

"I'm done with waiting. The only reward of patience is patience." His voice was dangerously soft.

The magical echo of the lyre chimed through her like flowing gold. Every part of her was willing, and so in harmony was he with her that no more words needed to be spoken.

He stepped closer. His hand gently drew away the hair that swept over her forehead. His head inclined slightly, and she saw that his gaze had narrowed drowsily. Already he was bewitched, and it was not of her doing. One hand cradled the curve of her neck beneath her ear; the other cupped her chin and cheek as his lips sought hers. "Give me your lips, Arrah," he demanded. "Let me taste the magic nectar of your mouth."

She could not refuse him; *this kiss,* she knew, was their destiny. Wantonly, her gaze summoned him full force. She would give him anything he asked for and more. Her fingertips, all nerves, lightly balanced against his hard-muscled chest.

Then he kissed her, a warrior's kiss. He kissed her as if she belonged to him, as if he had every right to her, every right to demand anything and everything from her. Under the pressure of his lips the heat and smell of him surrounded her. Every bone in her body, every fiber of her flesh, every facet of her femininity responded to his overwhelming maleness.

Though his mouth was warm, a shiver rippled through her, nearly unlatching her knees. Her lips parted, and his tongue, moist and hot, traced the inner softness of them. She opened her mouth fully, inviting deeper probing. He kissed her lushly and long, with a thirsty intensity that left her trembling with surrender.

A thousand years may have passed, kingdoms fallen, mountains been razed and oceans altered before he drew his mouth away.

His hands, strong and gentle, moved from her face to her shoulders; and wherever they touched her a flame streaked along her nerves. He paused at the neckline of her silken gown, slipping it slowly from her shoulders. Falling, it rustled like a chimera of tinkling faerie bells.

She pulled her eyes up and looked only at his face. In the half-light his eyes were as deep black as a netherworld abyss.

Then, he stepped back and removed his own garments. She regarded the sculpted contours of his naked body, running her eyes over his wide shoulders and continuing down to his narrow hips. Expectancy tingled through her.

He took her into his arms and eased her down onto a moss-softened spot beside the pool. She melted against his warm, bare skin, sliding her hands over his chest and twining her fingers around his neck. She felt his hand slide down, over her shoulder, then lower to caress the curve of her hip.

"You are beautiful, my lady swan," he whispered, and began trailing his lips down the line of her neck and shoulder. His thumb dallied around the budding spire of her breast. And then she felt sensation jolt through her as the warm wind of his breath and lips captured her nipple. Goose bumps shimmered over her skin. Her lips sought the silky softness of his dark head.

Little by little she felt his tongue preen the full circle of her breast. He nuzzled and lapped the furrow between and secreted his tongue's tip along the half-moon fold beneath. She sighed from the pleasure.

Terwen had said that the mystery of loving could not be spoken of, only experienced. Now, Arrah understood, for nothing could compare to what she was feeling. Near breathless, she felt the slick of his tongue inch across, intruding beneath the velvet tuck of her other breast. Unhurriedly, he tasted her plush swell. Slowly, spiraling, he drove her to almost beg him to capture her upthrust peak in the softness of his lips. When at last he did fasten firmly on her nipple, the force sent a shock of pure delight to her very fingertips.

Soon his head dipped down to rain hot kisses upon the hollow of her belly, and her desire spread like fever to tingle every nerve and cream-flushed pore. His dark head lowered, and his mouth met the inner velvet of her thighs. She relished the moist stroking as it moved up each leg in turn, debilitating her with desire. And then he was in her, tracing a fiery spiral within the folds of her moist flesh, tasting the small, sensitive confines. She felt light contractions as her virgin's channel expanded, readying to embrace his shaft. She ached with wanting.

She reached for him, clasping his thick hair in her fists and drawing his face up to her own. In the light she could see the flash of his teeth as he smiled.

"I'm dying for you," she begged hoarsely.

He kissed her full-mouthed; their waists met, her

midriff against his chest, his nipples against her fleshy breasts, their tongues probing each other.

He was strong, so vibrant in his maleness, so sure. But there was more to a swan maiden's mating than he knew.

She started humming softly. Her lips were at his ear, encouraging him as she opened her thighs fully to him and he slipped in.

Suddenly, he groaned full-throated as, powerfully, he thrust deep his shaft into the dark night of her fiery womb.

"Ahee!" he cried out as if a wild agony had seized him. He clutched her shoulders in momentary panic.

"Beway . . . beway . . ." she soothed. "I mean no ill to you. 'Tis the way with my kind. He who takes my maidenhead must pay such a passage. It will end. Then, I promise you a mating like no other you have known."

Traeth struggled for mastery. The power of motion seemed to fly from his limbs. All awareness drained to the ecstasy suddenly awakening within his shaft. It was as if a hundred lips were enfolding him. His body became one organ, hungering for her.

As he felt her nails dig into his shoulders, he plunged his tongue deep into her mouth. Her hips undulated in union with his, and soft moans crossed her lips. His strokes became more powerful with each thrust.

Between breath and sigh, he burst like a dragon spewing golden flame, overflowing with exquisite and exultant muscular force, strong and soft, potent and yielding, vulnerable in his every thrust.

"By the gods!" he shouted as he felt his power explode and his seed spill into her. Turbulent waves of passion throbbed through him.

Arrah cried out—a wild cry. And then it began: the explosion of constellations, a thousand stars bursting in her veins. Thick heat traveled from the center of her thighs like the silver moon's reflection multiplying on a glassy loch.

She felt melting surrender and full-bodied joy. An overwhelmingly blissful explosion rushed with delicious force in all directions through her body. She felt his heart pounding next to her own, and she held him to her with awe and wonder. Drawing a trembling breath, she lifted her head to seek his face.

His eyes were shadowy and shining. "Milady, your sweetness is beyond my imaginings." He kissed her forehead; he kissed her throat.

She smoothed his skin, running her hands down his back and over his buttocks. "To love is better than to dream of loving," she murmured.

"Mayhap we are in love's dream," he answered softly.

"Aye, we are part of a dreaming dragon's golden hoard . . . the most treasured, but also the most transient, part."

"Unfortunately, there is no longer a dragon."

"Nay, I think you are the dreaming dragon." Her hands cupped his head and she drew his face to hers, that his lips might touch her own.

He kissed her and then chuckled. "I am the guardian of this dragon's hoard."

"Is that why you chase off the halflings?"

"Aye, and everyone else who seeks to steal the wealth of dragon's gold. If the halflings were ever to ransack this hoard, 'twould be a great misfortune in the five kingdoms."

"So you easily slay all comers," she surmised.

"I know it must seem that way, but that is not the truth. Killing is never easy."

And in that moment she believed him. She looked at his face, no longer wary and closed, at the warmth in his dark eyes; and the unfamiliar touch of tenderness about him, existing for her and because of her, was enough to take her breath away. Even though she knew he was dazed with enchantment, she could abide in his arms forever and be well quit of the world.

She smiled at him, and the look in his eyes, steady on hers, set her pulses to leaping again.

The lyre issued a shimmer of notes, liquid, shining runs, holding the spell of love between them and enchanting the night away.

Chapter

7

Traeth refused to leave Arrah's side in the days that
followed. Entranced, he exchanged the companionship of the Fianna for intimate walks along the
lochshore or meandering rides into the forest with
Arrah. He plucked wildflowers for her, and with deft
fingers she fashioned them into garlands for their
necks and heads. He showed her his favorite haunts
beside the loch while she sang to him, weaving nets of
melodies that healed his spirit. Hour upon hour they
gazed into each other's eyes with absorbing tenderness, almost unable to speak for such longing. For
both, it was a time of open-faced happiness, a time of
drinking from the overflowing cup of love's enchantment.

Amidst the bliss, both were ignorant of ecstasy's
price.

One evening Arrah slipped off to be by herself. The
great hall was deserted when she returned—or at least
she thought so, until she heard Traeth's voice asking
mildly, "Where have you been?"

She stopped and stood motionless, then turned

slowly and dreamily to face Traeth. He stood with the light of the dragon hearth behind him, and he seemed taller than usual, and because his face was in darkness she might have been confronted by a towering shadow that reflected itself on the slate flooring in a misshapen, grossly exaggerated figure of darkness.

"I've been walking on the battlements. 'Tis a lovely night."

She moved toward him. He did not put out his arms to embrace her, but rested one arm on the lintel of the fireplace, the other behind him, and stared into the embers. She was silent. There was nothing she might say in the face of his apparent displeasure.

Instead, she walked over to the long trestle table, with its heavily carved legs that formed the massive taloned claws of a dragon, and sat down. The firelight shone across the table, the squat benches and beyond to the tapestries hanging on the walls, then finally disappeared in the shadows lurking in the tall corners of the hall.

"'Tis not safe for you to walk the battlements alone in the evening."

"I was not alone," she assured him.

"A tryst, Arrah?" he asked suspiciously.

Her only defense was to tell the truth. "Nay." She looked at him oddly, not understanding. "The Fianna stand guard. I felt quite safe."

"Safe. Hah!" he scoffed.

Taken aback, she said, "You've no need to be jealous of the Fianna."

"Jealous? I'd have a small opinion of myself had I naught to arouse my jealousy but the Fianna." He turned slightly, so that he might better observe her. "You look different," he went on, in the same accusing tone of voice. "Surely the moonlight did not put that becoming flush in your cheeks."

The flush became a hot flame, despite all she could do.

"You flatter me," she said, keeping her voice steady.
"'Tis not flattery that has given you that look of beauty."

"The outside air is invigorating to me," she tried to reason with him. "You have kept me at your side indoors the day long."

"Have I been so harsh with you that you must slip away in the dead of night? Did you fear, mayhap, that I might refuse to allow you the innocent pleasure of a walk?"

He looked back at the fire again, and she felt the tension rising in her throat like a great lump.

"Nay, I thought none of it."

"Is life so intolerable for you?"

Some instinctive sense cautioned her to best beware and humor him in this mood. "I have always enjoyed a walk," she said, "even in Myr."

"Mayhap someday you will ask me to join you. I, too, have a fondness for walking."

Uneasy, she knew there was more to his ill temper than her heedless conduct.

"We need to come to an understanding." He turned from the fire and fixed her with his smoldering black eyes. "You are mine and mine alone."

For a moment, too stunned to school her face, she could only stare at him.

He went on speaking in the deceptively calm voice. "I have been looking for you all my life, Arrah. Now I have found you, I won't let you go. I want you to share the rest of my existence. Is that so foolish a wish?"

"Nay," she said quietly. She clasped her hands tightly together and tried to breathe normally. "'Tis only that you are a warrior. You are sufficient unto yourself."

"No man can be that," he said, "and still be human."

He came closer and stood above her. Lifting his hand, he removed a blood-red ruby ring from his little finger. He took her hand in his and slipped the ring on her forefinger.

"The stone is a drop of crystallized dragon's blood, and very ancient. If you ever remove it from your hand, I'll consider the act a betrayal."

The air was stifling her, the fire burning her eyes with its unwavering heat. She was utterly confused, she could not think clearly; she wanted to retreat to the blessed privacy of the high battlement and find some measure of quiet in which to calm her shaken nerves.

"I want your companionship, your graciousness and your loyalty. You will be mistress of Rhune Castle. And every man in the five kingdoms will envy me."

Was he daft? Had he gone mad—mad with love? Aye, a sudden she knew that he had the love sickness. His pure love, for whatever mortal reason, had in the last hours succumbed to doubt and fear. He was caught in the dark side of enchantment; even in Myr, such things were only whispered about.

At the realization, a sickness of another sort gripped her insides as he stood by her, watching as she falsely admired the ring. It was her shackle, the price of enchantment's kiss.

"Come, milady," he said not unkindly, and offered his arm. She smiled, more ingratiatingly than she had intended. The distance to the stairway stretched interminably before her, but she walked it under his benevolent assistance.

Once in their chamber, she slipped from her gown and climbed into the yawning four-poster bed. His naked body was warm beside hers and despite his doubting and possessiveness the power of love was still between them.

Mayhap they both had the love sickness, she thought apprehensively. He had bewitched her, enthralled her, enraptured her. From the beginning, she knew she played a dangerous and risky game by losing her swan skin to his keeping. He was no god, in truth, or even godly. He was a man, a mere mortal, who wore a long sword at his side. He felt anger, loneliness and insecurity. He loved and hated as other men. Although he stood taller than most and held his dark head with the pride of a mage, he could die in a moment's time, like other mortals, and be reduced to bone and dust.

The thought of him dying brought a softness to her emotions. Aye, she loved him for what he was. A slow, delicious sweep of memory brought to her mind that first night of lovemaking between them in the dragon's cave. She reached for him and touched his cheek.

He caught her hand and pressed her palm to his lips. "Yours is the love I've longed for in my loneliness," he whispered.

She had never doubted this, and could not withhold herself from him.

What did it matter, after all? Love was love for the giving and for the taking. She brushed aside the tangle of his hair and smoothed the fine lines that life and battle had graven into his brow. Where her fingers went, her lips followed, moving from brow to eyelids, down sculpted cheeks to lips that welcomed her own like a thirsty man in a drought.

Terwen had said that no one knew a man like the woman who shared his bed. It was true. He was more familiar to Arrah than her own kith. He might be feared in the five kingdoms, he might be hated and despised by countless enemies, but in this moment, in this bed, she found him no threat. . . .

When Arrah awoke at dawn, she felt a vague apprehension, the more frightening and malicious because she could not immediately put her finger on the cause. Traeth still slept peacefully beside her. She raised her hand, stared at the ring of the dragon's blood and tried to think clearly.

What was she to do?

Beside her lay the man she loved, but his love was entrapping and stifling her. A ray of sunlight arched in a pale curve from the window to the bed, and flashed off the face of the ring. Even so, the day seemed all at once to be cold and dreary and infinitely melancholy.

Traeth stirred, his arms wound around her. Despite the uneasiness of her mind, she surrendered to his warmth. She clutched his strong shoulders, and all her disquiet began to dissolve to pool in urgent sweetness between her thighs. He was eager. Soon his soft lips were everywhere upon her body, brushing her skin until it tingled, tasting her like a man long starved. She moaned with desire.

Her hands slid down his smoothly muscled body as she opened her thighs. His gentle fingers stroked her, and all her cares melted beneath his touch. He stretched his length above her. There was no holding back, and he entered her as the stallion takes the mare, with strength and power. The power filled her until her spirit could hardly contain it. She gasped, her nails pressing into his skin, and he cried out a deep, husky release.

Radiance spun outward on a tide of pure ecstasy, pouring over her, through her in a blissful contentedness.

And all grew still. To the light of the dawning day, she opened her eyes and looked at his battle-scarred back and the smooth skin that stretched tightly over muscles honed by long hours of sword wielding. A shock of dark hair fell across his eyes as he turned his head to hers.

"Lady, may your life be blessed for the joy you bring me," he said softly.

And inwardly she assured herself, *Aye, he speaks*

sweet words and I've no need to worry. He may be a warrior and he may be possessive, but he's not that wicked. My loving will change him, truly.

"'Tis a day for hunting." He took a deep, invigorating breath. "I smell a fine hunt in the air. You shall ride with us," he declared, sitting up and climbing from the bed.

She swallowed back the impulse to decline, even though she was the one with the keen sense of smell and the air didn't smell any different to her than the day before.

After dressing, he left the chamber with the strict instruction that she must quickly ready herself and meet him in the courtyard.

Once there, the roar of male laughter and the yap of excited hounds greeted her. Traeth's mood was buoyant; there was expectancy in his face and warmth in his smile and dark eyes. She would never, she thought, understand the contradictions of his masculine nature. How could the thought of hunting so enliven him?

It was exceedingly difficult for her to watch Sib shadowing Camlan as he saddled his destrier. Sib had replaced her chain mail and sword with a small dirk that Dath Bright Spear had given her. It was clear by his manner that Camlan would not allow her coming. Even to the last, she remained underfoot until, whether planned or accidentally, he knocked her aside as he reined about his horse. Sib tumbled, scraping her cheek on the rough slate stones. Camlan offered no apology.

Once the word was given, the Fianna wasted no time mounting and spurring their horses forward. The hounds chased each other's heels over the drawbridge and the hunting party set off in a melee of gleaming flanks, tossing manes and rolling eyes. In truth, the air did throb, as if someone was beating a drum. It was not so much a sound—more an emotion of pulsing excitement and anticipation.

Traeth rode beside Arrah, and beside him rode Fergus Dry Lips, his red hair shining in the sunlight as rusty as a fox. Next to him was Bright Spear, with his long, braided beard dangling down like a whip.

"Are you sure we should be making all this commotion?" she asked Traeth. "Surely, all creatures know and will take flight at our coming."

Traeth laughed, shaking back his dark hair. "We are not rabbit hunting, milady. Our prey this day is more formidable. You shall see."

Mayhap I don't want to see, she thought but did not say as she rode along the track above the loch.

Now it becomes a morning of sunlit meadows stained red with heather and forests crowding the mountain slopes. She fell under the tranquil spell of the peace and quiet and the heart-shaking beauty of the green hills. Yet, she knew that, like the man riding beside her, this land could quickly become harsh and awesome.

His and this wild place shared the same nature, after all. He was forever fighting for possession. There was a dark heritage in his blood, that same heritage of violence and disquiet which had seethed through the haunted borderlands from ancient times. She wondered if that unrest in him, that dark vein of passion, must be guarded with a constant vigilance lest it stealthily conquer a man's soul and abandon him to that very same darkness he battled.

The company rode into early afternoon, paused for a short cheese and bread repast and then continued on again without spotting any game.

Then, a sudden, the lead hound gave tongue. The tangle of trees before them exploded into motion and the shaking branches became a great spread of antlers. A sleek body leaped out of the brake, while two hinds scattered in opposite directions. She heard the wisp of a spear hurtling past her ear toward the stag, but it fell short into the gorse beyond.

"Let leave!" commanded Traeth. His horse half-reared and he reined it back.

Beside Arrah, Enwir, Malicious in Battle, muttered with disappointment, "He'll not let us hunt the hind. Something to do with sorcery and the disappearance of his mother."

She looked over at Enwir oddly, knowing this was one of many mysteries surrounding Rhune Castle.

Arrah could hear something else crashing through the trees as the stag plunged away. The hysterical clamoring of the hounds focused on the new quarry and the pack poured up the slope in a swirl of flapping ears and lashing tails.

Traeth gave voice to another command that could not be heard above the yammering of the dogs, but Arrah saw him slash the rump of his horse with his reins and send it bucketing after the hounds. She gripped the mane of her own horse as it joined the pursuit.

She held up one arm to protect her face against the whipping branches while she held on with the other. All fell into confusion among the hunting party. The Fianna were hallooing the hounds and horses onward. The chase spread out, and the formation shifted as the bolder riders moved to the forefront.

She had no ambition to match such ardor. When she could control her horse again she reined it down and held it back to a careful jog that let her go around the obstacles—the noble stands of ancient oak and ash and the pillared aisles of pine, with their great girth; the thick undergrowth that in some places left little room to ride; and the enormous boulders, their faces softened by blankets of emerald moss and yellow lichen.

Their prey doubled back and forth through the

wood and once she caught a glimpse of something shambling across a clearing. This beast was like nothing she'd ever seen. It appeared huge and hairy, with tusks like a boar and taloned claws like a wildcat.

The hounds hung on untiringly while the Fianna rode along behind. They came to a drop-off, where the forest slopes plunged through great boulders down to a stream.

"It will seek to lose the hounds in the water," cried Bright Spear.

Her mount slid down the slope through the pines while the Fianna hurtled after the beast. She heard splashing as she burst through the trees into a chaotic tangle of horses and barking dogs.

She blinked at the sudden stench in the air and tried to see what they had cornered in the stream against a granite-faced cliff. Her pulse was hammering furiously in her ears. What faced her was no common beast but a weir, crossover spawned in old magic.

"Ho, here is the foe!" shouted Camlan the Unsmiling. "Shall we give battle?"

Flinching and feinting, the beast curled its tusked snout and let forth a rumble from its throat.

Arrah saw that the hounds held it encircled, the bolder ones darting into the stream to either side, where it caught them with long tusks and tossed them aside. One it grasped in its talons, crushing the body, tearing at sinews and cracking bones in its jaws. When it was finished, its gaping mouth was dripping blood.

The Fianna laughed.

Something turned over in Arrah's stomach and she drew her eyes away.

Traeth untied his javelins, then slid from his saddle and stuck the spears into the earth, ready to hand. Bright Spear was at his side, his spear ready. One by one the other men dismounted until the beast was surrounded by a barricade of dogs, horses and men.

Arrah moved her horse back.

The beast was not frightened, it was enraged—snarling, and holding its ground. The hounds surged in again, and she winced as a tusk ripped open a dog's belly. Blood reddened the stream.

Traeth reached for a spear and flung it. Its point bit, then bounced away. The air whispered with flying spear shafts as the other Fianna made their casts. The beast weaved and whirled; it dashed aside spear points and ripped at the hounds. Each attack fueled its rage, until a dark fury emanated off it like a tangible force. Arrah drew her horse farther back, away from the violence. Shouting, taunting and baiting like beasts themselves, the Fianna seemed undaunted.

"Stick it—hold it fast!" cried Traeth. The Fianna closed in; the beast whirled, caught in a truss of shining spears.

Traeth stabbed a thrusting blow to its heavy neck, and in doing so lost his balance. Bright Spear caught him and pulled him out of the way. When the beast lunged after Traeth, the Fianna threw themselves upon it. But being so powerful and ferocious, it ripped free and the men went sprawling. Traeth had regained his stance, however, and rammed his last javelin down the attacking beast's throat.

Arrah turned her eyes away; she could watch no more. She heard sounds of thrashing, screams of dying and curses of the still living . . . then all fell quiet.

She looked up. The beast's blood mingled in a crimson flow with that of the dismembered dogs.

The smell of blood, death and violence was so strong she became nauseous and was seized by dry heaving. She swayed in the saddle and would have toppled off but for the sudden support of the strong hands of Bright Spear.

"Lady," he said, "do not swoon. All is well."

"I . . . 'tis so much blood   " she tried to explain to him.

Then, Traeth was there, bloodstained and disheveled, his face shining with a great triumph. "Milady, you are a huntress now." Laughing with pride, he held before her a tusk. "Take it," he commanded. "'Tis your trophy." She shrank back as if he'd offered her poison.

Bright Spear advised softly, "Take it in hand, lady, or you will give insult."

Reluctantly, she took the tusk, abhorring not so much the object as the deed.

Turning back to the Fianna, Traeth said, "Butcher the beast, and give the hounds their share."

"The light is going fast," said Bright Spear.

"Aye," agreed Traeth, looking at Arrah. "We've a bit of a ride back to Rhune Castle if we're to get there before night falls. Lead out with milady Arrah and I will soon follow."

Gladly, Arrah turned her horse about, slipping the tusk into a pouch hanging from the saddle.

Bright Spear guided her up the slope. The climb began in earnest, twisting higher and higher, following no visible path, leading through scattered boulders. At the top she asked if she might take a moment to stretch her legs and relieve herself. Bright Spear halted, then held the reins of her horse while she slipped down and disappeared into the undergrowth.

When she remounted, she looked up at the treetops and saw that a high mist was descending, dimming the day. Below, she heard the snarling and bickering of the dogs fighting over the beast's remains. She still felt nauseous.

The way back seemed much longer. Mayhap it was because she did not recognize any landmarks in the mist that was closing in upon them. She kept close to Bright Spear, who was unspeaking. Turning her head, she tried to look for Traeth's approach, but could see no shapes moving through the trees. The moist air chilled her. The trees ahead dimmed as the mist cloaked them in white.

Minutes later, the mist was so thick there was no visibility. Arrah wondered what sixth sense kept Bright Spear going. An eerie silence fell all around.

Then, he halted his horse beside the trunk of an old rowan tree.

"Are we lost?" she asked.

"Nay," he said without elaboration.

Stiff from the long ride, she asked, "Can I dismount?"

"Aye," he said, dismounting himself and coming over to hold her horse while she slipped down.

"The light is fading fast. Mayhap we should make a fire as a beacon to the others," she suggested.

"Not here. 'Tis not safe," he said.

"Why?"

"We are caught in an in-between place—neither one place nor another."

"Then let us move on," she said.

"Nay, we will only wander night long. Here at least we have the protection of the rowan tree."

Arrah looked over at the trunk and saw the elusive shadow of the guardian tree spirit entwined amid the limbs and bark. Relaxing, she asked, "Are we to spend the night here then?"

"Aye," he said, giving her the reins of the horses. "Hold these."

He disappeared into the mists.

She heard rustling. When he returned, he emptied a heap of bracken from his cloak onto the ground before her.

"Make this into a soft pallet for yourself to sleep on," he directed. "I'll keep watch."

He unsaddled the horses, but left their bridles on and tied them to a lower rowan branch, where they nibbled upon the leaves.

Arrah settled into the softness of the bracken, refusing to take Bright Spear's offered cloak. "I've my own," she said.

He thrust a spear in the earth and sat down. Time passed. Arrah stared into the shifting mists and ruminated upon the brutality of the hunt. It had changed her way of seeing life . . . and men. She looked over at Bright Spear, wondering why she felt perfectly safe under his protection now, even though hours before she'd seen him commit vile savagery. His form alert, his eyes stared guardedly into the mists.

"What is it you watch for?" she said, breaking the silence.

"Creatures," he said.

"What kind of creatures?" she asked, knowing they had all night and if he chose to answer her every question in a single word there would be time enough.

"All sorts," he replied, and then to her surprise elaborated. "There are creatures that wait for wayfarers who become caught in the in-between. A lone man might be walking through the forest path and suddenly stagger as a night spirit mounts his back. Even though 'tis formless, its weight is immense, and there is no hope of shaking off the creature, for it breathes miasma, and croons abuse into the traveler's ear. By morning the poor soul is dead with exhaustion."

Arrah shivered and looked furtively in all directions, but all she saw was the gray blanket of mist. "Do you think there is any of that sort of creature nearby us?"

"Nay," he said confidently.

She sighed in relief.

"Nay," he repeated, "but there'd be other sorts."

"What other sorts?" she asked, hunching herself up uncomfortably.

"Creatures worse than that . . ."

"Worse?" She swallowed hard.

"Aye, worse!" he affirmed. "There is one whose name I cannot speak, for in the speaking it can be conjured. 'Tis one-eyed, livid-faced and long-clawed. It haunts the hills and crouches behind boulders, waiting for passersbys, which it flays alive with its sharp, curving claws. It eats the tender flesh, then takes the skin back to its cave to hang upon the cold stone walls as trophy."

Arrah had heard enough. She asked him nothing more, nor did he volunteer anything.

Throughout the night she struggled in and out of sleep, cold waking her to the haunting snuffling sounds just beyond. The tusked beast hunted her through her dreams, and Bright Spear's other creatures appeared in that otherworld through which she wandered. One-eyed, fanged and taloned, they reached out to slay her. And then she was not only the prey, but joined into the ranks of the predators chasing other beings through the wasteland, cornering and savaging them into shreds. . . .

"Arrah! Are you safe?" Strong hands closed on her shoulders. Still part vicious creature, she snarled and struggled against the unrelenting grip. Darkness weighted her closed eyelids like iron, and she tried in vain to free herself.

"Arrah, wake!" A slap stung her cheek and her awareness flashed open. She was biting Traeth's hand like a wild animal. "I've searched for you the night long."

Traeth was bending over her, his face all craggy planes and concern. Her jaws unclamped with the shock of her deed. He pulled back his hand, and she saw there a welling bruise. She reached out to him with remorse and attempted to speak, but her tongue would not form the coherent words of an apology.

The mists had dissolved and Arrah felt the awakening freshness of a light rain upon her face. The Fianna were standing by, quietly, as if there was something mightily amiss.

"We have him," another voice said, the voice of Camlan the Unsmiling.

Traeth turned upon Bright Spear. "You've betrayed yourself!" he accused.

Bright Spear's usually inscrutable features livened with righteousness. He bowed down before Traeth and said, "Milord, I did your bidding and escorted your lady. We became lost in the mists of the in-between place."

"I trusted you, Bright Spear," Traeth said coldly, drawing his sword. The Fianna all drew back, forming a square with the two combatants in the center.

Bright Spear came to his feet, a hand on his own sword hilt. "Milord, I've not besoiled your lady's honor. Give me fair judgment."

"My judgment shall be the edge of my sword," growled Traeth.

Arrah leaped to her feet and broke into the center, grasping Traeth's arm. "He has done nothing, but watched out for my well-being through the unfortunate night. I will not be the excuse for you to raise your sword against him."

Unmoved by her plea, he said, "The judgment is made." He brushed her hand from his arm and turned to Bright Spear.

In desperation, she caught him again. Her voice implored, "You are unreasoning. You've fallen victim to enchantment. You've the love sickness."

She did not miss the exchanging glances among the Fianna. Aye, they knew as well as she that their chieftain was bewitched.

He smiled disdainfully, an arrogant denial settling on his angular features and curving the corners of his lips. "Lady, remove yourself from this affair."

From behind her came Carne the Aged's quiet voice. "Stand back; you cannot stop him."

Weariness filled her as Carne's hand guided her

away. "Can nothing break this enchantment?" she asked him.

"Nothing but a look into the mirror of unmasking —though the shock of viewing their own darkness drives most men mad."

"Where is this mirror of unmasking?"

"Beyond the borderlands, in the Land of the Forever Young. Magh of Sidhe, the elven king, possesses it."

"I have heard of the elven king." The clang of steel on steel startled her and stopped her words.

She looked up to see Traeth and Bright Spear begin a ferocious dance. Traeth lifted his sword and brought it singing down. The edge grazed Bright Spear's shoulder.

Arrah swallowed her dread. Her eyes rose heavenward and she invoked the Goddess's protection upon both men.

Traeth's eyes were alight with animal keenness as he cannily stalked Bright Spear with his sword. But Bright Spear was a formidable foe, and countered Traeth's every swing and lunge.

Traeth moved with a power that was daunting, while Bright Spear had a fluid grace that allowed him to elude the mage's blows with apparent ease.

Arrah saw that something predatory was impelling them. She could not understand it. Wooing death, they reached out, then pulled back again, their swords ringing bitterly in the rain-sliced air. She looked at the surrounding faces and saw the same savagery there as she had the day before when they'd hunted and killed the beast. Their eager hunger for blood was once again exposed.

Fergus Dry Lips stood beside Camlan the Unsmiling, devouring each strike, while Camlan's eyes filled with the yearning to be in the fray. Even Carne's aged face had come alive.

Traeth strained with each lunge, and Bright Spear's muscled legs braced for every ringing blow. Harsh in

Arrah's ears was that ring, and her limbs winced. She cried out when Traeth's sword tip bit and blood gushed from Bright Spear's shoulder. The blood ran bright red over his chest, mingling with rain to spatter on the bracken.

"He's not fighting," murmured Carne the Aged at her side.

She fisted her hands, realizing it was true. Bright Spear was using his skill only to defend himself, while Traeth was going after him with dogged vengefulness.

Traeth struck again and Bright Spear's sword absorbed the blow. The two blades rasped together and held. Then Traeth thrust full force and unbalanced Bright Spear, who fell, rolled and came up in a crouch, his sword lost. Both men were breathing hard.

"I do not want to see your face again," Traeth said finally. Arrah saw no look of conquest in his eyes as he sheathed his sword.

Bright Spear looked back at Traeth, eyebrows knitting darkly, and said, "The love of this woman will bring you woe." He picked up his sword and sheathed it at his waist. His companions opened for him to pass from their midst. Jerking the reins of his destrier free, he climbed up into the saddle and with straight back rode off.

Arrah felt sorry for him, but she felt sorrier for Traeth and herself, for Bright Spear's words seemed prophetic.

Chapter

During the next days Arrah came to know her castle chamber very well.

She knew how many stones set the hearth, how many strips of tapestry draped the bed, how many steps from wall to window and back again. She knew by heart the hour, moment and second when the sun crept across the slate floor to illuminate the bedposts and leave in shadow the sideboard. She knew how the motes floated in golden rays and blurred at dusk and how the birds chattered outside her window at early dawn.

Each night she tossed and turned and lay awake in the long watches of solitude, and each morning she awoke, heavyhearted and despairing, to face another endless day of imprisonment.

She was no longer under the delusion that Traeth would ever give her back her swan skin. She had not seen him since their return, when he had secured her in the tower of the dragon's claw and left her. A page brought food and water once daily. The food she ate ravenously and the water she drank thirstily, but a wild thing as herself did not thrive in confinement. Her skin began to dry out for lack of bathing. First it flaked, then it cracked. The hairs of her head began to fall out when she combed it. Her eyesight began to dull.

No doubt Traeth was still under the spell, wandering that enchanted land where love coexisted with obsession. And in the after all he had never said he loved her. Aye, he blessed her, wooed her, seduced her—but never loved her.

Oh, there was no denying it. She was foolish to have kissed him, foolish to have believed he was not *that* wicked. Terwen had forewarned her, but she had ignored her counsel because she was curious and ready to explore a world different from her own. In doing so, she'd embraced illusion and hid her face from truth.

And so it went . . . until the midnight there came a knock at her chamber door. The unexpectedness of it left her paralyzed in her chair before the hearth.

The knock sounded again.

"Milady, I am without your door," came Traeth's low voice.

Arrah's emotions rose; she was very angry at him for locking her up and yet, she wanted to see him. "Enter if you wish, you have the key," she called out sullenly.

The latch lifted and he passed through the doorway. Arrah sat in her chair, enveloped in misgivings.

He seemed a stranger.

He smelled of mead and looked haunted. His hair was shaggy and his face shadowed with unshaven beard. His eyes flashed with dark intensity as he strode toward her menacingly. She wasn't sick, but the sight of him made her feel queasy. She clasped her hands together to keep from shaking.

He stood, staring at her as if he could no longer control the fever of possession that drove him. Stepping forward, he caught her shoulders and pulled her from her chair to face him fully. He embraced her, pressed his lips to hers, but she remained passive. A stone might have given him more response.

"Hah!" he growled. "Mayhap 'tis Bright Spear's lips you yearn for."

"Nay," she said soft and low. "I yearn for my swan skin and freedom."

He reached out and not too gently grasped her neck with his hand. "Arrah, you are mine, and I must protect what is mine."

"You protect me by imprisoning me? This I do not understand."

"I imprison you because I want you!" he declared. "Can you promise never to leave my side?"

"I cannot," she said truthfully.

"Then, I cannot return to you your swan skin."

Her lips tightened firmly. She said nothing.

Suddenly, the warrior, the part of him she could not abide, ripped her gown down the front, exposing her naked body to his view. She flinched and her lower lip trembled. Beneath his hot gaze her breath halted and her cheeks flamed.

"By the dragon's fire! You taunt me, woman!" His eyes bore into hers like twin pyres in which neither peace nor rest could be found. He grasped her shoulders as a drowning man might clutch flotsam. He bent his head and kissed her long, and vehemently. Again, she refused to engage, though every nerve and need of her body cried out with longing.

He drew back, visibly daunted by her lack of response.

"You are heartless!" His voice shook with passion. "Where is your warmth now that I'm enslaved by your kiss? Where is the woman that I lay with in the cave of the dragon's hoard? I cannot eat, I cannot sleep. I look nowhere but I see your face. In dream visions you haunt me."

"If you are so tormented by me, let me go free and be rid of my sorcery." She broke away and clasped her garment closed.

He caught her wrist with his hand.

"Never! If you try to escape me, Arrah, I will find you. I will hunt you down through the five kingdoms and beyond. I will slay any man who touches you and lay low any who give you aid." His nostrils flared. "You are no man's but my own."

He flung away her hand and left her. The reverberation as he slammed shut her chamber door echoed as loudly as thunder upon a mountain.

She flung herself down upon her bed and beat the bolster with her fists. For her the crystalline rainbows were gone; the sharing and smiling were gone. She was angry. She was angry because he'd stolen her swan skin and banished Bright Spear, whose loyalty to him was beyond reproach. She was angry because he'd torn her fine dragonfly silk gown and locked her in a tower. He was full of wicked deeds. How could she have ever loved him? Only through the spell of enchantment had she loved him, and now for her the enchantment was broken. It was a false love between false hearts. She didn't want to love anybody anymore, because it hurt to truly love.

A sudden her anger turned to tears, and she sobbed sorrowfully.

The days that followed were as foggy and unclear in her mind as the faerie mists that crept over the borderlands, veiling hill and loch. The face that gazed out the single window of her prison may have appeared calm and serene, but her heart twisted with pain, and she cried slow tears that welled from deep inside her, and gave no solace.

She thought about the nature of love and realized it was more a riddle than the riddle of men—though love, men and riddles all seemed to go hand in hand.

Terwen had said, "When you meet a man, as you see him, you will see yourself. As you treat him, you will treat yourself. As you think of him, you will think of yourself, for in him you will find yourself or lose yourself."

The sorrow was that she had lost herself.

She pondered more, wondering how she did see Traeth. At first she'd been fascinated by him, a man and warrior. Yet, the very warriorness that had intrigued her now alienated her. Was there a part of herself that could capture and possess someone against that being's will? Aye, by her very kiss she could! In truth, she had captured him by the kiss. She had asked him to kiss her, and he had resisted, until that night he'd taken her to the cave.

"Beway . . ." she moaned aloud when the magnitude of her deed struck full force. "What you do returns to you," echoed the words of the childhood rhyme.

Her next visitor came by stealth in the darkest hour before dawn. Magically, Sib appeared at the foot of Arrah's bed.

"Sib! At last." Arrah sat up in her bed, overjoyed to see that familiar form. "I've prayed you'd come. Why did you wait so long?"

Sib said nothing. Arrah lit a candle at her bedside and was shocked at what the light exposed. Sib's face was as bleak as a winter moor. Her eyes were forlorn, revealing more wretchedness than Arrah had ever seen before.

"What is it?" she asked, opening her arms to her sister.

As if dazed, Sib walked over and collapsed against Arrah.

"Tell me," she urged. "What has been happening to you in these days I've been imprisoned?"

"I have to leave," she whispered, low . . . so low that Arrah barely caught the words.

"What has happened?"

"He slapped me," she said softly.

Arrah winced, but it was no surprise, for Camlan's actions had been less than gallant all along.

"Again? I saw the first in the hall and a second in the courtyard," Arrah recounted.

"He asked me to hold a mirror while he looked at himself. He said, 'Hold it there; no, higher!' 'I'm too short,' I said. 'Give it to me,' he said, and abruptly took the mirror. My hand had been too lax upon the handle. When he snatched it, the mirror slipped from my fingers and fell to the floor. In irritation, he slapped me upon the head."

"That makes thrice," breathed Arrah sadly.

"I have to leave him now," she sighed, her face so downcast that Arrah's heart ached.

"Oh, Sib, 'tis true you must leave him now, for no swan maiden can abide such abuse a third time." Arrah tightened her arms around Sib, stroked her hair and said, "Mayhap, 'twas a good slap: It brought you to your senses."

"No slap is good, Arrah," Sib returned with hard-learned wisdom. "Why could I not see before? I'm ashamed of how I shadowed him day and night. I studied him. I mimicked him. What he ate, I ate. The sun rose and the moon fell and every moment he was in my thoughts. I wanted so to please him, but there was no pleasing him. He said that I must have six fingers to a hand, along with my other deformities. He called me a clumsy dolt," she said, tears falling in rivulets down her cheeks. "Why couldn't he love me like I love him?"

"Oh, Sib," comforted Arrah. "I do not understand these men. Mayhap being warriors, they have never learned to love."

"The mage loves you," said Sib, wiping her sniffles on her arm.

"He possesses me more than loves me. I do not believe that he loves me, truly. He is a victim of enchantment. Enchantment is not love. 'Tis ephemeral, ungrounded, grasping for glowing illusion. Like a mirror's false reflection, enchantment allows us to see only what we wish to see, and 'tis not the real thing. Because I am beautiful by the definition of this realm, Traeth believes he loves me. Because our bodies have been united, he believes he loves me, but we've not shared the sacred ritual of disclosure, nor have I sung my love lilt to him. Would he love me so well if I were like you and had not gone through chrysalis?"

"No, he would not," agreed Sib. "Are there men who can love a woman for herself and not for what they imagine her to be?"

"I don't know," replied Arrah. "That takes *real* love."

"And what is *real* love if 'tis not enchantment?"

"Real love is honesty," Arrah said succinctly. "Not only with the beloved, but with one's self. Real love is exposure and vulnerability, loving even though 'tis painful."

"How do you know all this?" asked Sib.

"I don't know it as much as I'm finding it out."

"I no longer love Camlan the Unsmiling," declared Sib.

"I don't think you ever loved him at all. You loved an image of a warrior. Is he not the most handsome of the Fianna?"

"Aye," said Sib sheepishly.

"You see, you loved him not for himself but for the ideal he represented. How could he love you for yourself, when you did not love him for himself?"

Through her tears Sib's mouth quirked with self-defeat. "Aye, I suppose I was the raven calling the crow black."

"Aye, I think so too. You must learn to value and love yourself before you rush into the world of men looking for a gallant hero. During chrysalis the inner changes will come, and from your experience here you'll be the wiser. In truth, we will both be the wiser."

"What will you do now, sister?"

"I'm not sure. This imprisonment is weakening me. If the mage is ever to truly love, the enchantment must be broken. Carne the Aged tells me that there is only one way, and that is for the mage to look into the mirror of unmasking. That relic is in the possession of Magh of Sidhe in the Land of the Forever Young."

"I think I know where he has hidden your swan skin," confessed Sib.

"What?" Arrah pushed back from her. "Why didn't you say so before?"

Sib sniffed defensively. "I . . . I thought that if you had it back then I would have to leave with you. I could not bear leaving Camlan. Please forgive me, Arrah. I've let you down."

Suddenly, Arrah was on her feet. If there was one hope in a thousand that Sib knew the whereabouts of her swan skin, they must search it out immediately. She pulled Sib up and asked, "Where? You must tell me now."

"Do you remember the night we were lost and found the bones?"

"Aye," said Arrah, noting the excited swirls in Sib's eyes.

"When they found us, Bright Spear said Traeth first searched the loch. Could it be hidden somewhere other than the castle?"

"Beway! You are right! The cave of the dragon's hoard! Of course he would hide it there, because 'tis a treasure of sorts." She looked down at the dragon's-blood ring upon her hand and said, "I won't be imprisoned another moment, Sib." With those words, she twisted the ring from her finger and tossed it onto the bed.

She was at the door before Sib could come to her feet. "You go first, Sib, and see if anyone is about. No one will question your moving freely through the castle. Give me a signal when the way is clear."

Sib slipped out the door as Arrah continued to whisper directions to her. "Open that small door to the battlements," she directed, pointing across the way to the adjacent door.

Sib knelt down and with the slightest of puffs unlocked the latching. She disappeared outside.

Arrah stood there in the darkness, leaning against the stout wood of the door. Her stomach burned nervously as she calculated whether this escape could be successful. She prayed that everyone was asleep.

Sweet as a linnet's call came a soft *whilloo*. Arrah sighed relief and started the stealthy journey from her chamber, across the battlements to the tower of the dragon's fang.

Outside, fresh air hit her nostrils like newfound life. She looked skyward and reveled in the morning starlight. She had been too long in that stuffy chamber, with no air or sunlight.

Sib was waiting for her at the battlement intersect to the tower of the dragon's fang.

Without an exchange of words, they ducked through the doorway and began the dark descent down the tower's spiral stairs. In the darkness, she was forced to use her hands along the walls. They reached the anteroom to the feast hall with no mishap. Then, with no warning, a great flood of light caught them, and they scrambled like cockroaches for cover behind shields and tapestries.

The door to the feast hall had been opened by someone. It was Fergus Dry Lips, who strode within inches of Arrah's flattened form in the shadows. Surely, she feared, he would discover her just by the loud pounding of her heart . . . but no, he walked on and up the tower stairs.

Sib slipped from her hiding place and into the feast hall. For some moments, Arrah remained pinned to the wall like a butterfly to a collector's board. Then she heard another *whilloo* and knew the way was clear.

The hall was deserted but for the coiling dragons of the great hearths. Their eyes glowed red in the carefully banked firelight, as if they were alive. . . . Suddenly Arrah's heart skipped a beat with the realization that in this time before dawn, they *were* alive! A shiver crept down her spine as she stood frozen to the spot. The dragon pair were the castle's guardians. What if they reared up and gave vent to their fire?

Sib motioned to her, but Arrah was paralyzed by fear. The distance across the hall, to freedom, stretched interminably before her. She had two options: to run screaming like a banshee or to walk slowly, step by step. Gathering herself, she chose to walk step by step beneath the glowering gaze of the twin dragons, praying all the while that she could overcome her fear.

Halfway across, from behind her she heard heavy footsteps on the stone flagging. Fergus Dry Lips was returning on his rounds. Her fear jolted and she jumped forward, running toward Sib, nearly knocking her aside as she shot out the threshold. Once outside in the courtyard, she drew a deep breath, pushed the lagging Sib forward and headed for the small door at the foot of the wall that would lead out of Rhune Castle and down to the loch.

Passing through this last portal of entrapment, Arrah stopped dead and turned to Sib. "Where is your swan skin?"

Sib's face clouded with confusion. "'Tis hidden. . . ." She looked about as if it were nearby. "I put it . . ." She shook her head with a shrug. Arrah realized that she was incoherent and disoriented because of the changes now happening in her young body.

Arrah studied her a long moment and muttered softly, "You've forgotten where you left it?"

Sib nodded.

She reached out and touched Sib's cheek. It was alarmingly cool. "Do your joints ache? Is your throat sore?" she quizzed hastily.

To both questions, Sib nodded again. "I've been eating huge amounts of food . . . fruits and greens. I can't get full. What does that mean, Arrah?"

"Oh, Sib, you're going into chrysalis. And it's too late to return to Myr." Even as she said this, Arrah realized that without her swan skin, Sib could go nowhere. They were marooned in this realm of men.

She turned and saw the curragh bobbing in the dark waters of the loch, then stared back at Sib. She dared not return to the castle. Mayhap, the safest haven would still be the cave. Taking Sib's hand, she led her down the winding path to the curragh and sat her down in it.

The water was shallow, and the curragh easily boarded. She unfastened the mooring rope and pushed it farther out until she was wading waist deep. Then Sib helped her to climb inside.

"Take an oar," she said to Sib as she took the other.

Sib grasped it.

"We must pull together," she directed.

The initial effort was a disaster, and Arrah decided they might swim more successfully—until she looked over at Sib and saw her slumped over.

"I'm so tired, sister," she confessed.

Arrah reached out and touched her temple. There was barely a pulse.

"Move aside; I can row it myself."

And so she did.

Straining, she at last reached the shore below the cave. She helped her sister from the curragh and up the boulder-strewn path to the cave's opening. She left Sib momentarily, then used her hands to grope her way through the arching mouth. It felt queer, and she smelled the faint odor of old dragon and gold. She searched the wall, feeling for the spherical form of an orb to light the blackness. She found one, and at her mere touch it flared bright.

A ripple of music from the lyre quieted her fears as she went back for Sib. Eyes glassy, Sib held Arrah's arm as they moved inside the lighted cave.

"So this is a dragon's hoard," she whispered weakly, sitting herself down on the mossy floor.

"Aye, the mage guards it."

Sib's face went distant as she listened to the threads of song. "I'm tired, Arrah. I'm going to sleep while you look for your swan skin."

"Once you fall asleep, Sib, you'll not awaken for one moon passing."

"Only that?" sighed Sib, yawning. "I feel as though I never want to wake up at all."

Arrah looked around. "You must secrete yourself here. Mayhap the cave is the best place for you to be, but not for me. I'll have to leave you alone. When you awaken, you'll remember where you've hidden your swan skin, and then you must go back to Myr."

Sib nodded drowsily.

Arrah looked around and spied a shadowed recess behind the pool. "Come," she urged, helping her sister up and moving her to a more protected place.

Gently she guided Sib down. "Dragon gold is not as soft as down. Are you comfortable enough?"

Sib murmured and curled up in a small ball.

Arrah repeated more instructions, but it was too late: Sib could not hear. She slept, the deep, deathlike sleep of transformation.

Arrah sat back on her heels and pushed her hair away from her face. Magically, before her eyes a whitish gauze cocoon formed around Sib's small body, and then a binding golden thread appeared, sealing the cocoon. One moon month would pass before Sib would awaken.

Now what was she to do?

Standing, she put her hands on her hips and surveyed the treasure chamber. The water trickled down into the pool and the lyre music, thin and delicate, rang through the damp air. She'd no other option than to begin searching for her swan skin in each chest and in each nook and cranny of the cave.

Time passed; the contents of every chest lay strewn about. Her swan skin was not there, but what she did find proved interesting. The dragon had a penchant not only for gold and those things precious, but for old, primal magic. In vessels and vials she discovered the elements that made the world restless, that encapsulated the essences of nature, animals, plants, winds, thunder, lightning, moon and stars.

No wonder Traeth of Rhune wore the mantle of the Mage of the Dragon's Mouth: He served as a guardian and guide to the knowledge secreted here. With these magicks she might harness the winds and waters and change her own and other people's shapes. She held up a tiny ruby-glass vial with a stopper the shape of a flame. One drop of this rare elixir upon her tongue might allow her to assume a myriad of disguises.

A sudden Arrah heard, above the lyre's tinkling, hounds baying far off. She set down the vial, rose to her feet, walked to the mouth of the cave and listened. As the sun dawned she realized that the air, which should have been alive with bird song at this hour, was strangely silent.

And then she heard the hounds baying again and she knew that the Fianna were on the hunt—for her. She turned around and picked up the vial. How else could she outwit the Mage of the Dragon's Mouth if not through disguise? The potions were clearly a way for her to turn this adventure to her favor. Naturally, as with all magicks, there would be risk. She might turn herself into a wee bird or a . . . She laughed outright at the image which filled her visioning. Aye, even the Goddess loves whimsy, she thought.

Arrah began humming softly the crone's song of her sisterhood. Carefully, she lifted the glass stopper and touched its tip upon her tongue. It tasted sweet, then bitter. In her mind's eye her disguise started to take shape, as her body began to melt into formlessness. . . .

Chapter

Arrah was gone!

Traeth knew she had left him as surely as if he had seen her die. He knew when he found the door to her tower room open and the ring of the dragon's blood cast off from her finger. He knew that from then on, every hour would be achingly empty, unless he found her.

"What do you mean the hounds can't follow her scent?" Traeth demanded, pulling back on the reins of his prancing moon-white destrier. The horse shook its cascading mane and shuffled backward as its silver-shod hooves thumped the wood-plank drawbridge.

Fergus Dry Lips, astride beside him, pointed toward the loch. "She escaped in the curragh. No hound can sniff scent in water."

For a single moment Traeth's dark eyes clouded as he looked out to the far shore of the loch. His anger rose like flames devouring dry kindling. How dare she leave him! How dare she remove the dragon's ring! Somehow she must have found where he'd hidden her swan skin, or she would never have escaped.

"I will ride alone in search of her. Until I return, you shall command the Fianna, Fergus," came his quick decision.

"Let her go," said Carne the Aged, coming forward on foot. His stern features were marked with emotion. "She is a wild thing. You cannot follow where she goes. You'll wander the spell-haunted borderlands, never able to cross over into the realm of Myr. Let her go, Traeth. I've not stood beside you all these years to have you fall victim to a faerie woman's enchantment. 'Twas your father's ill fate; do not make it yours as well."

Traeth leaned over until he was staring directly into Carne's eyes. The early-morning sun gave the old man's face an almost masklike appearance.

"I'll not rest until I find her. If need be I'll bring storm and raise gale so fierce that no creature can fly in the midst of it," he threatened, his eyes hard and uncompromising. And with that, he spurred his destrier across the bridge.

He rode. He rode all shaking thunder, and he felt not one whit better when he finally finished circling the loch and dismounted on the cliffs above the dragon's cave. His temper churned like rough seas as he entered the cave, but when he lifted aside the flat stone his mouth dropped open and his eyes widened with surprise. The swan skin was still there!

Traeth realized that without it she could not go far. But, he also knew, that would not prevent her from eluding him by hiding in the nearby forest.

He pushed the stone back and stood up. In the corner of his eye he glimpsed an oddity in the recess behind the pool. What was it? Taking a light orb in hand, he walked closer, peered down and saw a great ball of fluff. He touched it. It felt stiff, like marsh cotton or a spider's egg sack. Then he spied the golden threading around its center and realized it was a chrysalis. Strangely, something had chosen this cave in which to metamorphose. He'd found various creatures over the years in the cave, from wolf pups to owls, but never a thing as odd as this. Yet, in the borderlands such queer things could often appear. He would let it be and not destroy it.

Leaving the cave, his eyes were alert for signs of Arrah's passing. Like most of the Fianna, he was an excellent tracker, but he could not track through air. Luckily, she'd not found her swan skin, or he'd have lost her.

Even so, moment by moment he felt her escaping farther away from him. He must find her and bring her back, he told himself. Panic gripped him. She was a wild thing and knew the ways of the wild. She would be adept at secreting herself in the forest and hills, and because of her beauty no one would turn her away if she asked for help. Determined to thwart her escape, he decided to call forth a storm so great that it would waylay any traveler.

He stood on the cliff edge and began chanting a storm spell. Deep from his soul rose a low, fierce keening . . . a song that commanded winds and stirred the very workings of Earth herself.

Soon the rising wind whipped his cloak and hair and the clouds churned in the graying sky. Around him the silver zigzag of lightning stretched across mountain peaks, and thunder shook the air. A flash, the cutting crash, then a slow rumble sounded in the hills and rolled over the loch.

The workings of magic set in motion, he walked slowly and examined the ground for a trace of her passing. Here he found a footprint, there a single strand of golden hair. Her path was easily followed— almost too easily. She was going westward, toward the woods of the Two Swallows, beyond which lay the Land of the Forever Young and the abode of Magh of Sidhe. Apprehension gnawed at his mind as he thought of the dangers she faced. What if the halflings captured her as she wandered?

He mounted his destrier and rode west, with a chastening wind at his back and soon a wet, pounding rain upon his head. By the time he entered the woods of the Two Swallows the storm was full rage, bending the backs of trees to breaking and stripping branches bare of leaves.

Now, he himself needed shelter from the elements he had unleashed. He spied a stone hunting lodge in the forest and rode toward it.

Guiding his horse through the trees and into the coming darkness, he held his arm in front of his face to protect himself from the lashing branches. His horse turned sharply around an outcropping of stones and reared. Urging his shying horse forward, he knew he would have to spend the night there. He dismounted and led the horse into the cover of the lean-to behind the lodge.

The lodge was abandoned and overgrown with vines. Few passed this way. He shouldered open the door and stooped through the threshold. To his surprise, a fire burned in the hearth and an old woman warmed herself beside it.

Taken aback, he studied her a moment. She was a rag-wrapped crone, squat as a barrel. Her hair was stiff from dirt and grime. Her face was red and lumpy with warts; crooked teeth protruded over her wide lips, and yellow matter crusted her rheumy eyes.

"Many pardons, grandmother," he apologized for intruding. "Like yourself, I must take shelter from the storm."

"Och, please yerself, 'tis the hearth guest's right," she said.

Rubbing his hands, he moved near the hearth. The acrid smell of wet moss between crevices of rock was overridden by the rank odor emanating from the old woman. He shifted a little away from her.

"Where ye from?" she asked, tossing a branch upon the fire.

"Loch of the Dragon's Mouth," he answered.

"What's yer errand?"

She's a snoopy old hag, he thought with irritation. It was a breach of custom to ask a fellow wayfarer any more than was volunteered.

"My errand, grandmother, is not for your knowing."

"Musha, I *already* know," she snapped. Her fingers dusted her moth-bitten shoulder brat cloak as she spat into the fire. The phlegm sizzled in the embers.

"How could you? We've but just met," he said, eyeing her suspiciously.

"Musha, I'll have ye know I've the 'sight,'" she said, touching the corner of her eye.

"That may be so, but you've not sight enough to know when you should mind your own affairs."

"Och, ye're a touchy blaggard. Mind ye, I've sight enough to know ye've lost yer appetite over love," she said, reaching with an iron poker to stir the pot that simmered over the fire.

He bridled and his eyes narrowed. He did not like her. "Keep still your tongue, woman, or you'll be outside in the storm."

"Och, don't think to bully me. I was here first," she said with the impudence of a magpie. "I'll not give a sniff to that big sword you carry."

He glowered at her, but she merely grinned in his face. A hostile silence fell between them as he ruminated on his misfortune of cross-pathing with her ilk.

Arrah was ever in his thoughts, and now he allowed himself a full vision of her. He saw her changeling eyes and her golden hair, long and flowing. He rubbed the tips of his fingers together in an attempt to recapture the silkiness of its texture. He burned for her.

While she consumed his thoughts, he could look nowhere he did not see her. In his waking hours and in his dreams she wandered, a transitory spirit. He wanted her in his arms, against his body, her soft heat warming him to his soul's depths. The sultry musk of her scent lingered in his mind, as well as the memory of kissing the curve of her long white neck, suckling on the piquant sweetness of her lush breasts, and mounting the silken inner flesh of her parting thighs.

"Hah!" A sudden, he doubled over from a sharp jab in his chest. His eyes flashed open not to the vision of Arrah, but to the grotesque old hag's leering face and an iron poker at his throat.

"Wake from yer dreamin', ye bog-rottin' gander, and fetch us more firewood," she commanded.

Wholly stunned, Traeth stumbled to his feet and went out into the storm to do her bidding.

Once he was outside, the rain pelted him. Coming to himself, he wondered why he, a mage who could keep a fire going night long with a mere incantation, was out in the storm searching for dry wood?

He returned, stepped up to the hearth and faced the loathly lady, saying, "I'll see the fire does not go out. You can sleep."

Her rheumy eyes squinted. "I'll not sleep in a cold croft. Mind you, keep your word and cease yer dreamin'."

"I'll do just that if you cease your nagging," he returned.

"'Tis a big world. Ye can pass the night elsewhere."

"'Twould be my choice were there not a storm," he said, though a goodly part of him would have preferred to be out in the storm rather than keeping company with her.

"Do as ye like, but don't complain to me."

"I've not complained to you. You're the one doing all the complaining."

"'Tis my right, by age and happenstance." Then, in a groaning effort, she slipped off the stool, stretched her legs and shifted upon her side in front of the fire.

"I'm too old to be travelin' about the land and sleepin' upon stone floors."

"Why are you?"

"Och, look who's the snoopy one." She shifted again, then confessed, "I've met with misfortune."

Taking pity on her amid her muttered complaints about the difficulty of sleeping on cold stone, Traeth removed his cloak and lay it upon the floor to ensure her comfort. Mayhap it was his imagination, but in the watery depths of her furtive eyes he thought he glimpsed a spark of gratitude.

"What misfortune, may I ask?"

"Ye can ask all ye want. I'm not closemouthed like some. I'll not say names, but if the cap fits, wear it." She yawned a moment and continued, "I'm called Ghillie, Servant of Birds, though 'tis not my true name." She looked at him sidelong to see if this disclosure piqued his interest. "I was once very beautiful."

He thought, *Surely she is testing my gullibility.*

"There wasn't a maiden finer to be seen. I captured the hearts o' half the men in the kingdom. They was all after me, like they always be when a maid is fair-faced. . . . Ye need not smile. I know me hair sticks out an' maybe me last tooth will come out tomorrow, but 'twas not so long ago that I could have me pick of the heroes, until a wicked wizard cast a spell upon me and I had to wander alone."

He could not hold his tongue in the face of her blarney. "I suppose you'll want a kiss from me to break that spell," he said sarcastically.

"Ye shouldn't mock me. I'm good at cursin'. Ye might find yerself endin' up a wee toad in a stewpot."

"I humbly ask your pardon," he said, but his apology did not mask the waggishness in his voice.

She cleared her throat and spat into the fire. "'Tis not yer kiss I need to break the spell—'tis yer true love."

He let loose a guffaw. "Dear lady . . . 'tis my good fortune to love another."

"Ye couldn't be so cruel," she said, grimacing.

"Nay, cruelty has naught to do with it. My heart belongs to one woman and one woman only."

"Och, you sound a prisoner of love. What is this woman like?"

"She's a maiden as fair as you once were, and more."

"Do ye love her only for her fair face?"

"Nay," he said, trying to think why else he loved her.

"Go on. . . ." she encouraged.

"Hmmm . . . there are so many reasons I love her."

"Name some," she persisted.

"She's cheerful."

Ghillie's brows lifted lightly and she shrugged. "Anyone can be cheerful . . . even I. What sets her apart? Why is she special?"

"She's nice," he said, scratching his chin thoughtfully, wondering how much he might disclose to Ghillie.

"'Nice'?" echoed Ghillie, her tone somewhat disappointed.

"Aye, well . . . I've not known her very long."

"Where is she now?"

"I don't know. My purpose in being here is to find her."

"How did you lose her?"

Against his will, a despairing feeling rushed through him. He mumbled, "She left."

The words hung in the air a long time before Ghillie spoke. "There'd be more to it than that, I think."

"True, but I'm in no mood to blather on about it."

Ghillie sniffed. "Very well, I'll go to sleep. Mind ye, don't let the fire go out."

She turned over and promptly fell asleep, so soundly her own snoring did not wake her. And snore she did. Her jaw hung open wider than a booka's grin and the noise was more deafening than thunder rumbling through a hundred hills.

Traeth stared into the fire, his thoughts wholly focused on Arrah. Where was she now? Had she found shelter from the storm? A sudden he was engulfed in an uncomfortable flood of feelings that he was responsible for any hardship she might suffer. She was foolish to have fled, he justified. But he would find her, he vowed, no matter how far he had to travel or how long he had to search.

In the early hours of dawn the wind ceased and the rain stopped, but he was unaware, for inside the croft the storm still raged, in the form of the old hag's snoring. It was the whinny of his restless horse that brought him round. He prepared to leave straightaway, but puzzled over how he might free up his cloak from the hag's sleep-replete body.

Luckily, Ghillie awakened. "Be ye a-goin' now?"

The sound of her voice seemed almost pleasant compared with that of her snoring.

"Aye," he said. "I'll be wanting my cloak."

"Want all ye want. I'll be wearin' it as we travel."

"Hah! I'm traveling alone, dear lady." With that he reached down and yanked the cloak out from under her. She rolled dangerously near the hearth embers.

"Och! Ye're a divil in disguise to rip an old woman's spread from beneath her. I can see why yer lady left you."

Her barb stung him. He turned his back and strode out of the lodge before he lost his temper. He'd no need to be baited by an old hag whose only task seemed to be to make life a misery for others.

Outside, everything was white and still. In his anger he'd brewed up more than he'd supposed: It had snowed! Snow in summer! The line of the trees was solid white and a porcelain sun, thin and cool as a plate, hung above. Summer's growth stood mute in the unfamiliar white cloak of winter.

"Beway . . ." gasped Ghillie behind him. "What's happened?"

"Snow."

"Snow," she repeated wonderingly, and pushed past him.

"'Tis melting fast."

"All is covered, round and white and smooth." She reached and touched it as if she'd never seen the like of it before. Then, a sudden a great, thick pile slipped off the roof with a soft, muffled thud and covered her head to toe. "Begorra!" she squealed in a voice of rusty delight.

Traeth laughed heartily and began to brush her off. "You best return to the warmth of the hearth, grandmother."

"Nay, I'm to go with ye."

"Hah! Never! I've suffered enough in one night of your company."

She put her hands upon her hips and tried to straighten tall enough to meet his eye. "Without me, ye won't ever find yer lady love."

"How is that?" he asked, puzzled and a little amused at her odd notion.

"What if ye find her? Then what? She'll run from ye again at first chance. Ye can't keep her locked up forever."

He frowned. "How do you know I've locked her up?"

"I've the sight, I told ye."

"You know nothing of it," he dismissed, and turned away.

She caught his arm and challenged, "Why would you want a woman who doesn't want you?"

The question unbalanced him, and for a moment he couldn't answer. "She does want me," he defended.

"Why did she run from ye then?"

Traeth shrugged off her hand. "I need not tell you." He moved toward the lean-to, where his horse shook its bridle with impatience. He tossed the saddle upon the horse's back, unable to be rid of Ghillie fast enough.

"So ye're ridin' off without me, are ye?" she hollered after him in a high-pitched rail. "Here I be yer own true love . . . and ye can't see me fer yer false fancies. And there ye go traipsin' after one who cares naught fer ye. Ye palaverin' hound, ye can't smell what's before yer own nose."

Traeth spurred his horse into the woods, thinking her daft. He muttered on his way, "A man spends a single night beneath the same roof with a woman and she thinks your hers. She's a dotty one."

He rode on, circling carefully in hopes of finding Arrah's track. It was a clear, cool morning. The sun finally broke in the east and melted the heavy load of snow bending the long grasses. The bird chorus flowed on like a waterfall, over and under the quiet cooing of wood pigeons. The earth was slushy wet as his horse's hooves broke dark ground on moss and through bog.

It was a peaceful, undisturbed world, except for his own thoughts. Ghillie had unsettled him with her words. Why was he chasing after a woman who was running from him? *To bring her back,* came a clear voice in his mind. But another voice just as clear asked what he was bringing her back for. To be with him? To love him? Maybe, and maybe not.

Amid the doubt, a great knot of pain formed in his solar plexus as he rode. When Arrah left, it was as if he'd lost a part of himself. There was an empty place that needed to be filled, and he yearned for her, and only her, to fill it.

So the first night and a day passed. Sick with desire, he followed every track and byway, but found no sign of her. The snow melted. Sunset and moonrise came and passed. He did not eat, and drank little.

For two days he journeyed westward alone, cross-pathing with no one. At last he came to a river that marked the border of the Plain of Wonder and Sidhe. Toward sunset, just before the river mists began to set in, he heard the quavering, sweet sound of an old woman singing. Approaching, he saw the blue smoke of dry wood curl in the air. The woman sat beside the small fire, rocking gently back and forth.

"A tirra lirra to ye," she greeted. "What took ye so long?"

He felt his insides contract with shock and revulsion. It was Ghillie, Servant of Birds. He nearly turned his horse about and rode away. Yet, the warrior in him was determined not to turn tail in the face of a blathering old biddy.

"What are you doing here?" he asked, leaning forward on the pommel of his saddle.

"I'm a-waitin' for ye," she said glibly. "I've pitaties to share a-roastin' in the fire. Come sit beside me, luv." She patted a grassy spot.

He was not hungry, but he was weary and even a little despairing. "I'm not your own true love, grandmother, but I'll share your fire." He climbed down off his horse, removed its saddle and let the horse loose to graze.

"Uphill, downhill, ye took yer own good time in the gettin' here." With a stick, she popped out three smoldering leaf bundles from the coals.

He snatched one up and tossed it from hand to hand until it was cool enough to eat. With his dirk, he cut into the pocket and squeezed forth the steamy, pulpy mash.

"I've fresh herbs to sprinkle on it," she offered, pointing to a small pile upon a stone.

"There's not trickery in them, is there?"

"Och, ye don't trust me, I can tell," she crowed with delight. "Don't be afeard. I'll not force any love elixirs down yer throat. Ye must love me fer meself or not t'all."

He chuckled and shook his head, "'Twill be not at all, for I doubt I'll ever understand you, grandmother."

"Until ye love me, ye will never understand me." She wiped mucus from one eye and bit into her own potato. Talking with her mouth full, she said, "I desarve yer love."

He paused mid-chew. "You may deserve it, but I've none to give you. So be still about it and put something else besides love in that old head of yours. In your travels, have you seen or heard of the maiden I seek?"

"Aye," she said.

He straightened, and his eyes turned to her with his full attention. "What? Why did you not say so before?"

"Ye did not ask before."

She wholly frustrated him. He wanted to yell at her, shake her and be done with her, but he knew he must control his anger or she'd not tell him a whit about anything.

"So?" he prodded, setting his pitatie aside.

"So?" she echoed maddeningly, obviously relishing keeping him in suspense.

He spoke slowly, and with great effort maintained a level voice. "What have you learned?"

"A little here, a little there. I met a watching bird waiting for its family of rooks. It told me she passed by and asked direction."

"To where?"

"To the abode of Magh of Sidhe."

"Magh of Sidhe? 'Twould be very dangerous for her to travel there alone. What does she hope to gain?"

"Mayhap love, like meself," she said, giving a filmy-eyed wink.

He'd enough of her, and came to his feet. "I'll be taking a walk."

Disturbed, Traeth followed the river westward. The water had a life of its own; even as he watched, it reversed current with a white explosion of bubbles and whirlpools and spray. No one could swim the river, or sail it. Only the dead crossed the river into the Sidhe.

He worried about Arrah, feared for her safety. For a long time he stared as the last remnants of day slipped into the endless mists, and then he stiffened. He knelt slowly, careful not to make any sudden movements that might draw attention.

There was a group of figures coming through the mists. He squinted in the failing light and discerned five heavily armed halflings moving toward him. They were small and swarthy, with jet-black hair, crude features and sallow skins. Redcaps, he thought, one of the most evil of the borderland denizens. He knew that after killing, the Redcaps dipped their hats into their victim's blood. He had no doubt they were patrolling for hapless travelers along the river.

He rose from the tall grass and crept back to the fire, where Ghillie sat dozing. She was snoring loud enough to wake all of heaven and earth. It was too late to even smother the fire.

"Wake up." He nudged her gently.

"Och!" Her jaw dropped open in protest.

"Wake up, we've visitors."

The Redcaps approached and stood just beyond the ring of firelight. "A good evensong to you," said Traeth, eyeing the distance between himself and the spear he'd lashed to his saddle.

One, shorter than the rest, nodded, and said in a grating voice, "You are far from the main roads of the five kingdoms. Are you lost?"

"We are not lost," Traeth said, slowly moving toward his saddle as the Redcaps edged closer.

"Can we help you?" the Redcap asked, fingering the sharp tip of his battle hatchet.

"Mayhap," Traeth said, edging backward imperceptibly. "We are looking for someone?"

"A woman," volunteered Ghillie.

Traeth frowned, not wanting to give all away to these devils.

"Describe her," the Redcap asked, moving in close. The others did as well, and circled Traeth and Ghillie, cutting him off from his spear.

Traeth's hand slipped slowly upon his dirk. "You are crowding us," he said coldly.

"You are in our lands. We've the right to know your errand," the Redcap demanded.

"Why don't you put aside your weapons and we can talk like civilized men," suggested Traeth.

"Now!" the Redcap cried, raising his sword and lunging toward Traeth.

Throwing her brat over her head, Ghillie screamed and squealed like a sow at butchering time. Her full-throated crying disoriented the Redcaps long enough for Traeth to move.

For a moment confusion reigned. Traeth shouldered one Redcap aside and threw himself at another, knocking him down and wrestling from him a pike. With pike in hand, his attack lasted barely a hundred heartbeats before all but one Redcap had fallen at his feet in death's last agony. Terrified, the one fled, leaving behind the bloody remains of his companions.

By now Ghillie, as frightened as a child, was shivering beneath her brat.

"'Tis over," Traeth said, lifting the garment and peering at her.

"So soon?" A look of absolute amazement filled her eyes as she surveyed the bodies.

"One has fled, and we must as well. 'Tis not safe to remain here. I intend to cross over into the Sidhe."

"That is what I intend as well," she said, rising to her feet and arranging her brat tightly around her shoulders. "I'm told that Magh of Sidhe can break the spell upon me. 'Tis my last hope, since ye have spurned me."

"Hah! I'll not take you with me."

"And why not?"

"I must go alone."

"That is no answer!" she spat.

"There is but one mount, and two riders."

"Och! Ye'll not lose me so easily. Tell me this: If I were yer lady fair, what would ye do? Surely ye wouldn't abandon me afoot."

Traeth thought a moment and said honestly, "We would ride together."

"Good. I'll ride behind." She stepped gingerly around the bodies and walked toward his horse.

"Wait! I did not agree."

"Ye have no choice but to agree. We are companions of the road . . . and ye need me."

"How is it I need you? You are nothing but a nuisance." He gathered up the saddle and hefted it onto the horse's back.

"Ye need me to show ye a way across the river into the realm of Magh of Sidhe."

He tightened the girth straps and asked, "And how do you know the way in?"

"The watching bird told me."

"Mayhap, there is no such watching bird and you are leading me on a fox chase for your own ends."

"Mayhap," she grinned crookedly.

"Very well . . . you can come with me. But I'll not be responsible for your life and limb. You'll do as I say, when I say it."

"Och," she gasped, touching her heart, "ye're the kind of man to have."

Traeth wanted to swear. Muttering a curse or two under his breath, he boosted her up onto the horse and climbed on in front. Her arms circled his waist like a cat that had caught its prey. The devil, but she did smell at so close a quarter.

Stealthily, Traeth guided the horse into the darkness. For long hours into the night its hooves thudded over the soft earth. On one side the ground sloped away steeply to the river, on the other into a tangle of woods.

Once a large, black bird rose silent, soaring from a tree on ragged wings. It was all the life they saw.

"Is that your watching bird?" Traeth asked.

"Not mine, but a spying raven from the realm of Sidhe," she replied.

"You said you knew a way to cross the river. Now, where will that be?"

"The watching bird told me to seek out one called Modhan. He'd be a river guardian and human in every way but for a single eye in the center of his forehead. He'll carry us o'er the river into Sidhe, but only on a moonless night."

Traeth looked skyward and saw a tiny sliver of moon above the wisps of clouds. "It will not be tonight. How are we to find Modhan?"

"He will find us."

"He will find us?" Traeth repeated, doubtfully.

"Aye, if we stay by the river."

He yawned. "I see no need to ride on, then. I am weary."

Soon they dismounted in a copse of trees above the river. Traeth fed the horse and spread his cloak out upon the ground. He stretched full length, and in a short time Ghillie had moved beside him.

"You're too close," he said, irritated. "I've borne the stink of your person politely these hours past, but now we've no need to sleep side by side as well."

"If I were yer lady fair, ye would not send me away."

"My lady fair does not smell as foul as a bog in summer heat, nor does she snore like a rutting boar."

"Ye're a rudie," she grumbled, and scooted a little off. For a time she grunted, shifting this way and that to get comfortable.

Except for the sound of the river, it was quiet. Traeth allowed himself the luxury of settling back and relaxing. Arrah was always in his thoughts, one way or the other. He imagined her there at his side, safe and in his arms. He lay a while, gazing skyward, remembering Arrah's fanciful wish to touch a star.

"Look ye at the stars . . . they be so close ye might touch one," came Ghillie's noisome voice, spoiling his romantic thoughts.

The woman could annoy the very fleas off a hound's back, he thought sourly.

"See ye that one." She was pointing to a group of stars in the north. "It be the Cup of Heaven; see ye the bowl, the stem and the base. 'Tis the horn of plenty, of riches . . . of love," she said with such exaggerated feeling that he wanted to stuff her mouth with cloth.

"Do you think because we lay beneath the stars together I'm likely to fall under the spell of love? Not with you, grandmother. Keep your romantic notions to yourself, for they'll ever be wasted upon me."

"I think ye're a'ready under the spell o' love," she taunted. "But I'll give ye a bit o' me philosophy to ease yer agony."

"I'm sure you'll give it, whether I want to hear it or not," he muttered, rolling on his side, turning his back to her and musing that love's agony could not compare with the outright misery of sharing her company.

"If ye can't be with the one ye love, then love the one ye're with."

Her philosophy was hardly original, but it triggered a thread of an idea in his mind. What if he could break the spell by professing his love? At worst, it wouldn't work; but at best, it would transform her and perhaps prompt her to return to that place from whence she came.

He raised up on one arm and faced her. "If I went on bended knee and declared my love to you, would you let me sleep?"

She shot upright. "Could ye? I felt in me bones the time was ripe," she chirped, clasping her hands together as if her every desire was now to be answered.

He blanked his face. A jolt of repulsion streaked through him. "In truth, I do not love you, but sometimes the mere words can break a spell," he admitted, reluctantly.

Her sagging jowls sagged lower with disappointment. "The words must come from yer heart, not yer head."

"At least I offered. You'll find yourself another gallant in due time. Mayhap you would have better luck if you sought out a kindly man near your own age. I'm too young for you."

"Would ye believe it," she asked candidly, "if I told ye that I like men younger than meself?"

He smiled despite the necessity he felt of being firm with her. She did have a way about her. "Aye, I'd believe you. Just like I would like a woman younger than myself. Ghillie," he said, speaking her name gently, "I indeed understand your sad predicament, but we're mismatched."

"I've heard the more the mismatch the stronger the union."

"I've not heard that," he evaded.

"That's because ye're young and inexperienced. Ye need an older woman to show the how of it."

His smile became an outright laugh.

"What's funny?" she frowned. "Ye think I don't know the how of it?"

"I'm sure you know the how of it and more."

"Then what is it ye don't care for in me? Ye must tell the truth. Is it me looks?"

"In part, and the way you snore and spit. I'd be the laughingstock of the five kingdoms with you on my arm."

"But if ye loved me, 'twould make no difference what others thought."

"Aye, but I do not love you," he said, lightly but finally. "I feel no passion for you, Ghillie."

"Och! I don't think ye would know passion if ye bumped into it on the road. Ye're a swoonin' fool chasin' rainbows through a bog."

"Calling me names won't win my love," he pointed out, his voice soft and detached.

"Well, I'll not flatter ye, but ye'll have the truth from me. I'll not play courtin' games either. It's funny entirely that when a man thinks a woman is after him, he's off like a hare, but if she doesn't care a rap, och, he'll give the nose off his face to get her."

"Mayhap, you should play hard to get," he advised.

"'Tis not honest. I'm easy to get," she confessed with a pathetic sigh. "My heart is ever out there. 'Tis part of the curse of me bewitchment."

An unbidden empathy filled him and a startling tenderness crept through his outward guard. "In the all, Ghillie, I suppose we do have bewitchment in common."

"Beway . . ." She made a murmur in her throat of muted sympathy as she straightened her skirt over her knees. "Me sight told me that was the truth of it. Ye would not chase a woman who did not want ye unless ye were bewitched as well."

"'Tis my own folly." Regret seared his voice. "Knowingly, I kissed the lips of a swan maiden."

"And why?"

"She wanted me to." Traeth's senses melted involuntarily, craving the pure pleasure of her kisses once again. The dull ache of wanting her was more potent than ever.

"I think 'twas more than that. I think ye wanted it

as well. Ye wanted the heady elixir of enchantment. 'Tis normal, but not true love."

"You say not, but then what is true love, Ghillie? It can't be your ceaseless pandering and pestering."

"Aye, 'tis not. It could be our task to discover the answer together."

He stared at Ghillie. She was looking back at him from cloudy eyes, and yellow matter clung in a paste over her lids. Her face was ugly and old, marred by warts and wrinkles. Until now he'd not chosen to see past her queer features. But there was suddenly more, a certain knowing. . . .

"Mayhap, Ghillie," he answered, a peculiar smile on his lips.

"Tirra lirra," she sang gaily, "'tis a beginning."

Chapter
10

Somewhere in the unfriendly borderlands, there was one friend. He appeared the next moonless night. Modhan the giant was twice as tall as Traeth and well-muscled. He was human in every respect, except for the single eye set in the center of his forehead. But for all his huge size, he was gentle and unassuming, and waited outside the ring of the firelight until he was noticed.

"Halloo," called Ghillie when she spied him.

Traeth looked up from his task of sharpening his sword on a whetstone and took Modhan's measure, then rose to his feet and walked over to meet him.

After a brief exchange, Modhan came within the ring of firelight and approached Ghillie. He touched his forehead and bowed to her with grace and gallantry. She gave him her gnarly hand, and he pressed his lips to it.

Traeth thought it odd for the giant to show such favor to the ragtag Ghillie, but he was learning that there was more to Ghillie, Servant of Birds, than met the eye.

"Your watching bird spoke right. This is our man Modhan. Are you ready for adventure, grandmother?" said Traeth, a sparkle in his eye.

"Not the sort that'll leave me throat cut and me gullet wavin' in the wind," she replied, scratching her side.

"What is your errand?" asked Modhan.

"To enter Sidhe," explained Traeth.

"I can carry you across the river, but after that I cannot protect you," spoke Modhan, his voice oddly soft for a man of his size.

"'Tis enough," said Ghillie.

Modhan led the way down to the river edge, whose swirling currents seemed impassable, even to Traeth.

"I will carry the man first," Modhan said to Ghillie, "you second."

"What of my horse?" asked Traeth.

"Aye, him last, though he will not like it."

He stooped. Traeth climbed upon his broad shoulders and he stepped down into the frothing waters of the river. It was green and churning and icy cold. The waves washed over both their heads. Traeth breathed water and foam, burning the lining of his nose. Something scratchy and slimy, like the long fingers of goblins, grasped at his legs. Modhan kept himself upright, though there was something pulling him down, a pressure that would not cease. Fear gripped Traeth; he believed they would both drown in the gulping torrent.

Modhan strained, but powerfully moved forward and climbed the other bank. Gasping, Traeth was dumped without ceremony upon the ground. His great chest heaving, Modhan returned to the river and disappeared into the froth and foam.

Traeth lifted himself on one elbow and saw Modhan finally emerge on the other side, lift Ghillie upon his back and sink out of sight again. Long minutes passed before the head of Modhan rose from the river.

"Och!" Ghillie was choking and coughing. "I be drowned," she groaned, water bubbles gurgling over her lips.

Traeth was on his feet, helping to get her sopping body off Modhan's wide back. "Nay, not drowned, but clean, Ghillie. You've had a bath at last. 'Tis not all bad, this adventure."

"Beway," she shivered, "nary a soul should suffer such an ordeal."

Modhan said nothing and returned to the river to fetch the horse. Traeth pushed Ghillie's belly so she might expel the water she'd swallowed. All the while, her teeth chattering, she moaned and whimpered.

"You needn't have come," Traeth reminded her, lifting the tangled wool of her hair and wringing water from it.

"Och! Nor ye yerself!" she spit back, pushing him away and sitting up.

"I wish you'd stop bawling. It might draw the halflings to us."

She shut up, but only for a moment. "Begobs! Look at yer horse," she said, pointing as Modhan rose out of the river.

Traeth turned and blinked his eyes. The white horse was now black. "Aye, we've crossed over into the magical realm of Sidhe, to be sure. What was white is black and what was black is white."

Sweat rolled in silver pellets from the pores of Modhan's forehead as he released the frantic horse. It stumbled and lurched before gaining its balance. Traeth caught the bridle and calmed it with a few words.

Modhan lowered his long-shafted limbs onto the ground to rest beside Ghillie. His one eye traveled over her with caring tenderness that belied his fierce visage. She was still shivering. He reached over and rubbed her limbs vigorously, not touching her intimately but taking pains to be gentle.

Traeth watched, fascinated as she preened to Modhan's attentions. He did not understand it. Only minutes earlier, she had rejected Traeth's efforts to minister to her.

Over the next hours everyone slept in the sun and dried out their clothes. When Traeth awoke, he found the giant sitting beside the still-sleeping Ghillie, just staring at her face. It was odd, thought Traeth.

"What do you see?" asked Traeth, kneeling near him.

"I see innocence, purity and a rare beauty. Why would you bring one such as her into this realm?"

"Your one eye must see what my two can't," Traeth remarked, unable to fathom Modhan's attachment to Ghillie. He shrugged. "She wanted to come; I could not shake her. She seeks a lover who can break the spell cast upon her by a sorcerer . . . or so she says."

Modhan's single eye left Ghillie and pinioned Traeth. "Do you love her?"

Traeth uttered a snort of disbelief. "No," he said flatly, "but I'm beginning to like her."

Modhan laughed quietly. "Well, it's a start."

The giant rose to his feet. The movement awakened Ghillie, and she sat up with a yawn wide enough to expose the insides of her toes.

"I'm leaving you now," Modhan said.

"Beway," she breathed, so sadly that Traeth thought she might shed a tear for the giant. "I'll miss ye."

Go with him, then, thought Traeth, wanting to be rid of her. But he held his tongue in the face of Modhan's obvious adoration of the old woman.

Modhan turned and, lifting a long arm, pointed beyond. "There lies the Plain of Wonder. You must cross it to find Magh's domain. It is full of illusions and specters, but take heed: Never sleep where you have drank or eat where you have prepared your food. Fare forward and fare well."

With that, Modhan stepped back into the river to

brave its vicious currents once again. Traeth looked west to the Plain of Wonder, challenged by Modhan's admonition.

A cool wind rolled crimson clouds across the sky. It was not yet evening, but already the western sky blazed with sunset. Only in Sidhe did the undersides of clouds glow bloody.

Traeth first heard the baying of the hounds from afar, echoing over the plain, growing louder and wilder, and containing the unmistakable howling of blood lust.

"Quickly, Ghillie," he said, kicking out their supper fire. "We cannot sleep where we've eaten."

"We've not even eaten yet," she protested.

"I wager we will not sleep at all, from the sound of those hellhounds," he replied.

Lifting Ghillie in his strong arms, he mounted his horse and spurred it westward. He pressed on until he reached a barren, rocky incline that rose sharply above the plain.

He leaped down onto the ground and unfastened his spear from the saddle, then thrust the tip into the earth. "You stay upon the horse, and if I fall, ride on."

"Mayhap, I will ride on before ye fall," she said with a wry mockery in her voice.

"Ghillie, I want none of your blather. Stay near, for you may offer a hand up if need be."

Three hounds appeared suddenly, racing across the plain toward the outcropping. The horse reared, nearly throwing Ghillie off, but she gripped the reins and held fast. They were huge beasts, standing near as high as the horse. As they ran, red fire shot from sharp-fanged mouths and their paws struck sparks from the stones. Their eyes were wild, lolling moons, burning with malignant intelligence. One beast pulled in front of the others and leaped for Traeth's throat.

Traeth threw himself down and raised his sword

point high. The great hound lunged onto the blade, yelping and writhing. Blood-specked saliva spattered Traeth's face and body. Before he could yank back his sword, a second dog raced forward. Its jaws clicked shut barely a blade's thickness away from Traeth's throat. Ghillie intervened, whipping the air with the rein leathers and screaming a battle cry fierce enough to momentarily startle the two other hounds, allowing Traeth to reach his spear.

Again, Ghillie entered the fray. In her gnarled hand she had been holding a large, round stone, which she now threw into the face of the second hound. It snapped and swallowed the stone whole. Suddenly, it stopped and gasped. The hound stood twitching, then rolled upon its side and lay still, its sides rippling in the throes of suffocation.

The last hellhound Traeth took down with a spear thrust deep into its dark heart.

"Has it ended?" asked Ghillie, with barely enough strength to hold back her snorting horse. She stared down at the last fitful agonies of death.

"Aye, for now." His chest heaving, Traeth flashed her a hero's smile. He wiped his spear upon the grass. "You must be grandmother to the Morrigan. Even now, your face glows with the battle light."

"Och! More likely me face glows with fright light," she said frankly. "'Ere's yer hand up, and let's be off."

He took her hand and hefted himself upon the black destrier. They traveled some hours in a fading light that tinted the ground red. At length mist began to form, veiling everything. He wondered if they should halt until the morning.

Suddenly, the horse's head jerked up and the animal shied and sidled. A soft glow of red appeared in the misty air. Figures moved around the light, muted and unclear. Traeth raised his spear.

"Halloo," croaked Ghillie.

"Hush!" he commanded, clamping his hand over her mouth. She bit it, not so hard as to draw blood but hard enough to cause him to flinch.

"Keep yer hand to yerself. Ye'll not silence me if I want to speak!" she reproved.

"Be still!" he muttered. "You'll give us away by your chatter."

"They know we're here. We might as well be cordial."

The disagreement between them became moot as the mists parted and revealed a wonderful sight. Riding toward them was a company of women—beautiful women cloaked in scarlet. Their red-gold hair shone like flame in the twilight; around their necks wide torques of twisted gilt gleamed, and the bridles of their gray horses glittered with rubies.

The leader rode forward a few paces and smiled at Traeth, her eyes bold and welcoming. "Hail, Mage of the Dragon's Mouth," she said in a voice like wind sighing through the corries. "I am Pryn, daughter of the thousand-year queen, Fan Fach. If you follow, you will find a haven of welcome."

Taken by their nobility and beauty, Traeth spurred his horse forward.

"Och! Are ye really so heedless as to follow them?" questioned Ghillie. "Their naught but a bunch of weir-women."

"If I do remember, you were the one who called 'halloo,'" countered Traeth. That silenced her, but only briefly.

He rode behind Pryn. The others moved alongside, riding straight-backed and graceful.

In time they came to a clearing. A great crimson tent was pitched on the misty ground. Pryn dismounted and stood before the tent opening.

"Stay with me this night," she said softly.

Traeth nodded and climbed down off his horse.

"I'll be yer guest as well," announced Ghillie, scrambling to follow Traeth.

Within the tent were piles of furs and rugs of silk such as Traeth had never seen. Blazing sconces filled the tent with warmth. The light shone on vessels of gold laid out amid a sumptuous repast. The beginning beat of drum and rattle of tambourine drew Traeth's attention to the other women, who were lounging on pillows or sitting before great drums. He was a man alone among beautiful women . . . except for Ghillie beside him. She sat hunched, a dowager chaperon. Once or twice he saw her reach out for a piece of fruit that she secreted in the folds of her brat.

A dancing girl in gauzy skirts, her midriff bare, swirled in the center of the tent. She whirled and pirouetted, twirled and stamped. His eyes focused on her gold-ringed ankles and swirling crimson skirts, wholly entertained by her brazen movements. Her hips jerked in quick thrusts and her cream-white shoulders shimmied her breasts with wanton abandon, evoking an erotic heat in Traeth's groin. He needed a woman—but not any woman would quench the fire of his desire, and this flaunting woman only made his need worse.

Behind him, Ghillie mumbled under her breath, "You'll not find yer true love here . . . or have ye forgotten her so soon?"

Her reminder was redundant. Nay, he'd not forgotten Arrah. His eyes searched the faces of all the women around him, fruitlessly seeking those eyes, those lips, that face that was Arrah's and Arrah's only.

"I've got to relieve meself," said Ghillie, coming to her feet with a groan.

Ignoring her, Traeth reclined upon the blue-black fur in front of the food and entertainment. As usual, he'd no appetite and, oddly, the food before him looked little better than Ghillie's roasted pitaties. He did not partake immediately, preferring to watch the dancing.

In a whirl of silver, a different dancer appeared. She was veiled and moved more delicately than the other dancer, with her bawdy movements and exaggerated gestures. The drums slowed to a sensual beat and the high, lilting tones of a flute augmented the pulsing rhythm. The dancer lifted her hands, following the curves of her body skyward, and swayed to the music. Her movements were fluid, languorous and melting. Her breasts quivered beneath the silver-threaded silks like rolling waves at sea. Tinkling beads and lank tassels lapped against the round of her swaying buttocks.

Traeth watched her, his dark eyes lambent and absorbing. Loose silk folds revealed her rounded breasts, and her skirts clung between her legs so he could see the deep cleft of her thighs. He felt desire rising like never before; he wanted her to be Arrah, and for a short moment pretended she was.

Savoring her, his eyes followed the line of her long, slim legs, the curve of her hips, the swell of her breasts. He swallowed back the desire that had consumed him for long days and nights, the wild, lusting heat that ever simmered within him. He wanted Arrah, with her opal eyes and honey voice.

He pulled his gaze away, circling the lovely faces of the women around him. But none could satisfy his craving, his desire, but Arrah.

He looked back, and the dancer in silver was gone. He felt the familiar fierce desperation of loss and the gaping hole in his chest that could only be filled by one woman.

Ghillie returned and sat down beside him. "Ye look as if someone has stolen yer favorite fribble."

With an expression that disguised any trace of feeling, he said, "Mind your own cooking pot."

"Drink." Pryn offered the cup to Ghillie first.

Ghillie accepted, drank deeply and then belched. Traeth held up a hand of refusal to the proffered goblet.

Pryn's glowing eyes traveled over him with the prurience of one who knew all mysteries. She looked at him quizzically and spoke in a tone spiced lightly with affability. "Dear me. Does nothing tempt you?"

"All tempts him," answered Ghillie. "But luckily, he's a'ready bewitched by a fair maiden afore ye."

A hot unspoken look between the two women did not wholly pass Traeth by. There was a short, unfriendly silence between Pryn and Ghillie that he attempted to rectify by humor. "Aye, a man can only take so much bewitchment."

Pryn's golden eyes studied Ghillie, and then she said, "You look tired, grandmother. Feel free to sleep. I think the mage can take care of himself. I don't blame you for trying; I'd do the same myself. The effort was fine—it's just not going to work."

It was clearly a threat, however courteously posed, and for some odd reason it did not sit well with Traeth. Ghillie was his companion of the road, and one stood by one's companions, whether he liked them or not. He'd not be here without her help and courage during the attack of the hellhounds. This and Modhan's admonition not to sleep where he had eaten prompted him to make a quick decision.

Ghillie was yawning, as if Pryn's very words cast upon her a spell of sleep. And then she let drop her cup. He moved to her just in time to catch her in his arms as she fell back under a powerful wash of drowsiness.

"What was in the cup?" he asked Pryn.

"A sleeping draught, of course."

"You had no need to do that. She is old and sleeps easily on her own." He rose to his feet. "We'd best be departing on our way after all. I thank you for the goodwill, but as I said before, a man can only take so much bewitchment."

He caught Ghillie up, supporting her, and she leaned against him, her senses suspended. She wasn't heavy for him, but she was solid, and he felt the narrowness of her stooped shoulders and the hump of her bent back.

"Do stay. . . ." begged Pryn, her planned seduction obviously thwarted.

"Nay," he returned, "'tis no use. She's a ruthless snorer. We'd find no peace the night through, believe me."

He ducked out the tent and hefted Ghillie upon his horse. "Hang on," he said, mounting behind her. She swayed precariously on the saddle.

"I've been poisoned," she said, rocking back and forth and groaning.

"Nay, it's only a sleeping draught."

"I'm sick . . . truly sick."

"Ah . . . that sort of sick." And he did the kindest thing that he could do—supported her as she heaved over the horse's neck.

No one in his experience had even been sick with the full-bodied misery that Ghillie was now. She moaned and groaned with the ballyhoo of a cow stuck in a bog. After she'd recovered some, he traveled on with her through the night. It wasn't until the wee morning hours that she settled some and dozed against him in the saddle.

As he rode, he glanced down at Ghillie, cradled in his arms. In her face he saw old age at its most ruthless. She was ill, coarse and spent. Her skin was wrinkled and warty and hung in loose wattles from her chin. But oddly, he felt an attachment to her and wanted to keep her from harm's way as best he could.

In the shifting white fog that hung on the morning

air, he entered a stand of blossoming hazel trees. In a gardenlike setting beneath the trees, a spring bubbled from moss-bound rocks. The hazel blossoms burned in glowing, vibrant colors; no insect or bird flew about the trees, and nothing crawled about their roots.

He brushed Ghillie's wrinkled cheek with his fingers and whispered gently, "Wake, grandmother. 'Tis time to stretch our legs and rest."

Her narrow eyes opened and she let loose a sputtering breath that nearly knocked him off his horse by its foul potency.

Hastily, he dismounted and helped her down, then released the horse to graze.

"Och! Me legs is pudding," she gasped, walking unsteadily. "'Tis awful to be awld."

"Mayhap we've the spring of youth," he said, kneeling to drink. Beside the spring, fastened with a silver chain to a stone, was a silver bowl.

Ghillie moved beside him. "Is it safe? I'll not drink just anything. I've learnt me lesson well."

"I'll drink first and you can see what happens to me." The water rose and fell in a graceful arc as he filled the silver bowl. The liquid flowed down his throat like ice, with a delicate, almost perfumed taste.

"Well?" asked Ghillie after a few minutes had passed.

"'Tis very refreshing."

"Good. I see no wee toads popping out of yer mouth, so it must be safe." She did not wait for the bowl, but dipped her hand in the sparkling water and drank from her cupped palms. "'Tis sweet as honey, this water."

"Aye," he agreed, drinking more as if he could not get his fill.

"I feel better a'ready," she remarked, sitting down upon the grass. She plucked a flower and sniffed it. "Me bones no longer ache, but I'm feeling sleepy."

"You've had a hard night. I'm tired as well. I think we should sleep and then move on." He yawned and put down the silver bowl.

He lay back, breathing deeply. Strange thoughts flashed across his mind's eye: warriors fighting beastmen; great armies clashing on hilltops. Faces flickered before his eyes, men and women with arrogant countenances. And then the single face he most sought to see solidified before him—the face of Arrah of Myr.

"Traeth?"

Her voice rang softly in his head and, although the image had not moved her lips, he knew she had spoken.

"Arrah . . . you are here," he said hesitantly.

"Aye." She seemed to regard him with some amusement.

"How did you come here?"

She laughed, a light, tinkling laughter that reminded him of the Lyre of *Guivre*. "I've been here all along. You choose not to see me."

"I would never choose that," he denied.

"Nay." She lifted a golden brow in challenge. "But you have."

"Were you the silver dancer in the tent of Pryn and the scarlet women last night?"

"Through your enchanted eyes, I was." Her mosaic eyes studied him kindly. She was beautiful, a marvelous perfection of features.

He felt agony. Last night she'd been within his reach and he'd not realized it. "Arrah, come back with me now."

"I will not." Her voice echoed as if from a great distance. "Not until you see me without enchantment's illusion."

He brought his fingers up to his temples as if trying to hold together the clouding vision of her.

"Arrah . . ." he cried out, but she was gone. "Heaven be damned!" He cursed the dream that had brought him face-to-face with the woman he loved, for now he awoke emptier than ever.

Opening his eyes, he found himself staring up into the sky, and he lifted his hand to shade his face from the sun's hot glare. A cry of shock caught in his throat; his voice seemed to catch and rattle. His hand was shriveled with old age. He sat up with difficulty, for his joints were stiff. Looking down at his hands, he saw that they were papery and spotted brown, with cracked yellow nails like Ghillie's.

The truth hit him like a physical blow: The spring water had wrought a transformation upon him. Clumsily, on his hands and knees, he crawled to the spring. The weight of his chest armor dragged on him.

"Sorcery be damned!" he swore when he saw his reflection. His smooth skin was wrinkled, his thick chestnut hair gray and sparse. His sight—his perfect sight, which could send an arrow flying right to a target's heart—was dim. And his hearing, which could catch the fine call of dunlin across the loch, was dull. Now, he barely heard the gurgle of the spring, close as it was.

A shadow moved across his reflection. It was Ghillie.

"Och!" she cried out. "Och, ye've aged one hundred years! Ye ignored Modhan's warning and slept where ye drank."

"'Twas the spring water." His voice sounded hoarse and unfamiliar to his ears.

"But I drank as well," she protested. And then she began to laugh, a crowing cackle. "Mayhap when ye're as awld as me ye can get only younger. We be a pretty pair, and not so mismatched now . . . me own true love."

He wanted to choke her words right off her withered lips, but he hadn't the strength.

She might have guessed as much, and knelt beside

him, putting one of her soft hands upon his. "Och, I'm being unkind," she soothed. "I've forgotten the shock of me own transformation. To be young and then awld within ten heartbeats is beyond reason's grasp. Me face took some getting used to, even to meself."

Traeth nodded, running his hand over his balding head. "I understand now why you are so cantankerous. My body feels worn out. I can't see or hear beyond my nose."

"Aye, awld age is a trial to the young of mind. But 'tis not the end of life. The spell can be reversed if we find how."

"Let us hope we find how before we both die of old age," said Traeth, turning away from his reflection. He felt more compassion for Ghillie now.

A sudden he looked up, and surrounding him was a party of horsemen, black-clad knights on black horses that were shod in gold and dressed in golden bridles and golden saddles. He shouted a warning to Ghillie, and reached to draw his sword from its sheath, but he'd not the alacrity. Ghillie moved faster and made for the spear.

The horses moved skittishly, their hooves turning the earth. A single rider leaped off his horse and caught Ghillie's hand.

Traeth called out hoarsely with as much force as he could muster, "Let the woman be."

Another rider halted his horse before Traeth. "Grandfather, put your weapon down."

"I'm no coward," Traeth declared, bravely raising his sword with two hands. "I have fought demons and beasts and men, without flinching."

"No doubt," the black knight answered dourly.

"Take his sword, before he hurts himself," chuckled another.

Traeth's lips tightened with the frustration and shame of his inability to defend Ghillie and himself from these warriors. "Who are you?" he asked sternly.

"We are guardians of the fountain. Anyone who drinks that pure water must earn the right. You must face one of us in hand-to-hand combat."

"Troth!" declared Traeth. "I have drank a'ready and have been cursed for it!"

"Still you must fight," the knight said, lifting his lance to readiness.

Traeth straightened as best he could, thinking he would soon die and be the better for it. At least he would die a warrior, as he had lived. He clutched his sword weakly, schooled his face in pride and stepped forward.

"Nay," cried Ghillie. "Ye cannot think this to be a fair fight. We are strangers to yer lands, and as guileless as snails crossing a glen. We seek the abode of Magh of Sidhe. He's expecting us. Ye'll raise his wrath if ye do harm to our awld bones. What honor is there in battling an awld man who cannot see past his nose?"

"I don't need your meddling, Ghillie," said Traeth, taking an unsteady step forward.

"Do ye want to die?" she cried.

"Hah! I'm near dead already," he returned.

A sudden the black knight ended their debate by dismounting his horse and moving to stand in front of Traeth, then pointing his lance tip level with Traeth's heart.

"Be challenged!" Traeth roared, and swung his sword with a mighty grunt. The impact broke the knight's lance, but Traeth, unbalanced by the effort, fell to the ground. After a stunned moment, he rose to his feet and hefted his sword in hand again.

The knight drew his own sword.

Back and forth under the blossoming branches of the hazel tree they wielded their swords. The fight was slow; determination marked Traeth's every swipe, while the knight halfheartedly engaged him until Traeth could no longer lift his arms.

The black knight retreated and sheathed his sword. With a half-bow to Traeth, he said, "'Tis a draw in courage, to be sure."

Ghillie rounded on them both, scoldingly. "'Tis a draw in foolishness." She shrugged off the hand of the knight. "Ye'll be taking us to Magh of Sidhe now ye've finished yer play."

"Lady, why should we do this?" asked the knight.

She put her hands firmly on her hips and asked, "Why should ye not?"

A soft laughter rippled through the surrounding knightly troop at her audacity.

"What say you, brothers?" asked the black knight.

All nodded favorably.

Then, bowing to Ghillie, the black knight said, "'Tis a full day's journey to the palace of the elven king, Magh. Let us ride."

Chapter
11

At dusk the troop of knights crested the rise above Magh of Sidhe's domain and found themselves looking down on the crystalline palace of the Forever Young. The sun was sinking behind translucent walls, reflecting over the golden turrets a myriad of colors—it looked as if a thousand rainbows shimmered there.

"'Ere we be the forever old in the Land of the Forever Young," said Ghillie, a wry edge to her voice.

Traeth made no comment, as his thoughts were on the likelihood of encountering Arrah. Had she found her way safely here?

As he neared, he could see and hear a sudden flurry of activity and a flash of sunlight on banners, and then the huge golden gates opened. Richly clad knights astride golden-bridled horses, splendid hounds, bards and harpers and fine ladies were gathered in a spacious courtyard. The ladies inclined their graceful necks at Ghillie and him.

He knew the elven race was powerful and that knowledge sometimes created great fear in mortals. Before the boundaries between Sidhe and the realm of men were formed, the two races, faeries and mortals, had known one another well. Yet the knowing had never been straightforward, and the adventures that mortals and faeries had together had been fraught with uncertainty. He was learning himself that the love that could exist between the two races might turn to hopeless longing.

Ghillie squinted against the sinking sun. "What will they do to us?"

Traeth's arms still supported her as she sat before him upon the destrier. He said to her ear, "We have nothing to fear from them; they are honorable. And we are too old for them to take much notice of."

The faerie host lined up at the palace steps and some touched their hearts, but most stared at the spectacle of the two aged persons.

"Ye are wrong. They do notice us . . . and see, their eyes are full of pity," said Ghillie.

"Mayhap envy. To remain forever young means to remain forever the same. What is the benefit of that?"

"Och," she said. "Ye been awld but a few hours and now ye're a graybeard philosopher."

He chuckled. "Not unlike my childhood guardian, Carne the Aged. He taught me to make the best of life no matter what was set upon my platter. How he would laugh to see me older than he is himself."

"Aye, he would at that," said Ghillie.

He looked at her oddly. "You speak as if you know him."

"Och, in my awld life I've known everyone," she said, and looked away from him.

The courtyard came alive with torches, banishing the dusk. A tall man, slender in the way of some elves, stepped into the light. "My Lord Magh bids you welcome and awaits you in the hall. There is food and drink prepared and he bids you break your fast, rest and refresh yourselves."

The man held the horse while Traeth slowly eased

himself off. They helped Ghillie down, and on unsteady legs she and Traeth struggled for balance against each other.

In the elegant hall, there was merrymaking. Faces shone radiantly in the firelight. Elfin lords and ladies sat along trestle tables laden to overflowing with exotic fruits, ambrosias, nectars, sweet confections and delicacies of every sort. Looking around, Traeth admired their polished crowns and glittering jewels. Pipes and harps played leaping melodies while maidens in floating gowns danced in the center dais.

He took Ghillie's hand and held it securely. "Have no fear, Ghillie, I'll watch out for you."

"Did I say I was afeard?" she asked, hobbling alongside him down the wide stairway. "Ye treat me like a featherhead. Ye forget I was awld before ye and fared very well on me own."

"I meant only to assure you," he defended.

"Assure yer own self more the like," she grumbled.

"Listen to us," he said. "We're a pair, bantering back and forth as prickly as white whiskers, and there is the king of Sidhe watching."

Magh of Sidhe, proud and gleaming and wearing a crown ablaze with gems, sat at the head of the assemblage on a great throne. Beside him sat a woman, lily fair, with hair of red-gold and as beautiful as dawn.

"You will be Traeth of Rhune, Mage of the Dragon's Mouth," he said, and his high, rather light voice floated clearly above the clamor of the hall.

"I am he," Traeth replied, "and this is Ghillie, Servant of Birds."

"Aye, I have expected you both."

Traeth's head turned with interest. And then his interest faded and his brows knit in a gray line. Suddenly, he felt a sharp pain. He reeled unsteadily and clutched his heart.

"What is it?" Magh of Sidhe rose to his feet. "Bring

a chair," he commanded. He stepped close and supported Traeth's elbow. Two bearers quickly brought a silk-cushioned chair and he was helped to sit down. "Are you all right?" asked Magh, his sharp eyes full of concern.

Traeth shook his head and muttered, "Nay . . . nay. 'Tis a sorry end to come to after all. I drank from the enchanted spring and now I'm old and I'm dying."

"He's got the love sickness as well," enlightened Ghillie to Magh on the aside.

"The love sickness? How came you by that?"

"He kissed a swan maiden," replied Ghillie.

"I can speak for myself, Ghillie," Traeth interrupted, still breathing laboriously.

"No ye kin't. Ye're a-gaspin' fer yer last breath. If ye'd quit thinkin' of yer own true love, yer heart might settle a bit—otherwise ye'll die before ye see her," she scolded.

"Ask him if she's here," Traeth pressed Ghillie.

"Who?" asked Magh.

"The swan maiden," said Ghillie.

"Nay," answered Magh, scratching his chin and keeping a thoughtful eye steady upon Traeth.

The disappointment was a breaking point for Traeth. He'd lost her. His eyes glistened with moisture.

Ghillie knelt down beside him and stroked his shoulders. "Och! 'Tis not the end of life. Ye'll find yer lady, trust me. Now dry yer awld eyes and make yerself decent."

"Why did you undertake such a perilous journey and dare cross into Sidhe? What is it you want from me?" asked Magh in a quietly regal voice.

"He's come to find his lady love," she enlightened as she patted Traeth's shoulder. "Meself, I've been enchanted and must find one who will love me for meself."

"And how is that to happen, Servant of Birds?" Magh asked, his eyes glittering in a strange way.

"I know not," she said, rubbing her warty chin.

Magh's face was unreadable for a long moment, and then he smiled, betraying his noble features with a flicker of mirth. "'Tis easily solved for both of you," he said with easy resolve.

"'Tis?" asked Ghillie with a plenitude of doubt.

"You do not see it yourselves?" he quizzed, as if even a wee babe might discern it with clarity.

"Nay," admitted Traeth, "I see nothing, but then I'm near blindness."

"You"—he pointed a slim, graceful finger at Traeth—"you came to seek your lady love, while she"—his finger shifted to Ghillie—"has come to find one who will love her for herself. 'Tis simplicity itself. Your wishes are most compatible. I decree that the two of you shall wed . . . here this night in the palace of the Forever Young."

"Troth!" Ghillie chortled with delight. "I've me heart's desire!"

Traeth was not so joyful. "But Ghillie is not my true love, high king."

A spirit of a smile still lingered on Magh's lips. His face held fleetingly the telltale softening of mischief. "She soon shall be. I will have your vow to wed her, that she may be freed from this unfortunate spell which binds her. And you yourself may benefit . . . though 'tis true you are old, and said you are dying. But take heart: You can do one last good deed before your death."

"Aye!" chimed in Ghillie with unconcealed enthusiasm.

Traeth frowned, his gaze straying to the nearest portal of escape. "Beway," he said in a soft plea. "I'm an old man. Once the spell is broken, Ghillie will be repulsed by me."

"Only if ye act repulsive. Love is love," clarified Ghillie, out of patience.

"Come now, have foresight and see the good and justice of it all. Make sacrifice," Magh urged gently.

Traeth looked over at Ghillie and let loose a resigned sigh. "I should have known from that first night you would persist and have your way with me."

"I'll make yer last hours pure bliss." She shoved her face within inches of his until the sourness of her breath near eradicated him on the spot.

He looked at Magh, then spoke his reluctant acceptance. "Be quick about it, before the groom becomes a corpse."

Magh of Sidhe reached for their hands and joined them in his own. "Beneath sun, stars and moon come together you two who wish to pledge your vow to one another. Blessed be."

The faerie woman stepped to Magh's side. In her hands she held a drinking goblet of beaten gold, the face incised with flowing glyphs and tiny semiprecious stones set around the rim. She pinched a single drop of juice from a rowanberry into the bottom of the goblet and swirled it slowly about. Magh passed his left hand across the rim and touched each of the gems in turn, bringing them to sparkling life. And before their eyes the goblet filled.

Magh took the goblet and lifted it to his lips, then passed it to Ghillie. She drained it in a gulping swallow—or thought she did, for when she passed it on to Traeth it was full again.

"Och, 'tis overflowing," she said. "Drink ye and pass the bride cup on that all may benefit from the juice of life."

The cup moved through the hall as one and all sipped its endless overflow.

Releasing their hands, Magh said, "May your eyes be always open to each other. May your hearts overflow with endless love as the bridal cup."

"Shall we kiss then?" asked Ghillie with an expectant smile that appeared almost sweet.

"As you choose," returned Magh.

Traeth looked at Ghillie, but in the all and all he could not bring himself to kiss her. So, she kissed him, upon his wrinkled cheek.

A cheer went up through the hall.

"Alas!" cried Ghillie, holding out a hand and touching her face. "I've not changed a bit. I'm still awld. 'Tis not enough to wed me—you must love and bed me."

Traeth fell back upon the chair, overwhelmed. "Dear lady, you have high expectations. I can do no more for you."

"Aye," said Magh kindly. "Milady, you are a rose in winter, and must not expect to blossom in summer's heat. Be patient and abide at his side."

The pulse of his labored breathing had become so loud in Traeth's ears that he could hardly hear the exchange that passed between Ghillie and Magh.

"Patient!" grumbled Ghillie. "I'm too awld for patience."

"Is he not your own true love?" asked Magh.

"Not so true as I thought or I'd be meself once more," she pouted.

Magh's gaze rested upon her with a tolerant smile. "No one can see the end from the beginning. Surrender to the fates, milady. . . . Now you both should leave us. I've a chamber especially in readiness for you." He raised a beckoning hand to his strong-armed servants and they came forth to carry Traeth upon the chair from the hall. "Go then."

Ghillie followed, clasping Traeth's hand. "I'll not leave ye," she promised, her voice brimming with renewed devotion.

They were taken down a narrow, meandering corridor through a gardened courtyard and past a gushing marble fountain. From above came the coo of doves and the shimmering song of a nightingale. They passed into a large room aglow with pearl lanterns. In the center was a bathing pool. Sculpted alabaster sylphs poised around the pool between white pillars that shouldered the arching roof. Flower petals were strewn on the glossy floor and climbing roses and vines entwined around the pillars. Most eye-catching in the room was a tall, golden-gilded, black-sheened mirror.

The bearers set the chair down. A servant laid out a rich array of elven clothing and bath linens on a low table, while another pulled sheer panels of gossamer curtains, enclosing the area in privacy. All bowed and left Ghillie and Traeth alone.

" 'Tis a faerie palace, to be sure, and I'm wed to thee by fairy oath," bubbled Ghillie. She plucked a red rose, inhaled its fragrance and stuck it in her matted hair, then reached for an apricot and bit into its soft flesh. "Do ye think that pool is for bathing or just looking?"

"Bathing," he said with certainty.

"Then I shall bathe," she announced.

"Tell me how warm the water is," said Traeth, still lying weakly upon his side. "I'll not make the effort unless it will take the chill from my bones."

Ghillie stepped over to the pool and dipped her fingers in. "Ah . . . 'tis very, very warm. It might do ye good. Mayhap 'tis a magic pool and will restore muscle to yer spindly legs and color to yer sagging flesh."

"I've nothing to lose," he said disparagingly.

"Nothing," she agreed with a shrug. Her manner was congenial. "I'll help ye undress."

Her hands were sweetly warm where they touched him in a calm, sexless undressing. She lifted his tunic over his stooped shoulders, assisted him in pulling off his leggings. Oddly, he did not feel self-conscious about his deteriorating body in front of Ghillie. The moment between them was companionable and held a rare, easy intimacy.

Kindly, she said, "If ye slide yer arm over me shoulder I'll help ye over to the pool."

Once he stepped into the pool, he stopped aching. He felt the heat of the water glide over his skin and warm his body. The warmth permeated his limbs and tranquillity settled on him.

He looked up and invited with feeling, "Come in yourself, Ghillie. 'Twill be as close to heaven as we'll get at our great age."

She laughed, that laugh that had at first so annoyed him, but that now was familiar in its mirth. He lowered his eyes, giving her the privacy to undress.

Gingerly, she eased her old bones into the pool and let loose a slow sigh.

"How does it feel?" he asked.

"Good." Then, with a knit brow: "But I'm still old and withered as a prune. Alas, these wrinkles aren't from sitting too long in the water, to be sure."

He chuckled. "Mayhap old age is a gift." His humor was aimed at cheering and instilling optimism.

"Och, to be old before ye're old? I see no gift in that. 'Tis like dying before ye die."

He moved to take her hand, which lay gnarled and curving in his as he then touched it gently to his lips. "And that is the bright side, Ghillie, my companion of the road, that as long as we remain in the Land of the Forever Young, we'll not age a second more."

"Och, but ye still can die. I suppose ye think that single thought and a kiss on the hand is going to cheer me old bones up. It doesn't." A brief smile bloomed and faded away as she glanced over at their entwined hands. She watched curiously as he stroked the tip of his forefinger over the curved surface of her nail plates.

His expression was soft. "I suppose you think that my becoming old is just deserts for my rejecting you."

"'Twas a harsh lesson, but I'll not deny ye weren't desarvin'.'"

He lowered his eyes. "Aye, I was, and more."

"Do not be too hard on yerself. Ye are changed for the good."

"How do you mean?" he asked, finally releasing her hand.

"Ye are gentle as I've not seen ye before. And ye're not as piny over yer lady fair."

"In truth, you are right," he admitted. "Just sitting in this pool with you by my side has brought me a contentment I've not known. I no longer feel the incompleteness or yearning I did before, and I think my appetite is returning."

"Mayhap ye have what ye need, but not what ye want," Ghillie mused.

He chuckled. "They say the wanting is always better than the having. Now, I'm too old to have and too wise to want."

To Ghillie, his words held the ring of disillusionment. "Well, whether we want it or not, we've one another."

They stared into each other's old eyes for a long time. His glistened with that last vestige of aliveness granted to the aged.

She was not sure who moved to whom first, but her arms were soon around his neck and his hands around her waist.

"Awld Ghillie," he whispered affectionately, then kissed her cheek.

She felt the power of that kiss from her cheek to the very ends of her graying hair and beyond. A sudden, her heart warmed with the gentle vibrancy of his sentiment.

She drew back from his arms and smiled wonderingly at his face. "Come now, 'tis time I showed you something."

He gave her a curious stare, but raised himself out

of the pool, albeit unsteadily. She left the pool as well and fetched linens to dry themselves on. Slowly and carefully donning the delicately sewn clothing, each dressed. She supported his elbow and urged him to stand before the dark-glassed mirror.

He waved an arm and shook his head. "I've no need to see myself," he said, refusing to look.

"Ye must look, Traeth. 'Tis the mirror of unmasking. Ye must see yerself as ye truly are, without the illusion, and all enchantment will be broken."

"Nay," he resisted. "I would rather remain an old man than see the utter darkness of my soul. All know one look in this mirror can turn a mind to madness."

His body was trembling.

"Only if ye are mad a'ready. Ye are a warrior! Ye have faced death in a hundred battles! Now, by the gods, have the courage to face yerself. Look!" she commanded, stepping aside.

Ever so slowly, he raised his eyes to the mirror. The lightless surface lent his thin, aging features a ghastly appearance, like one long dead. Aye, he *was* dead. His body was cold and unfeeling.

The mirror coalesced into a shifting, eerie semblance of his form, which then paled and shrank back into darkening depths and reemerged as infinite multiplying images of black shadow. The shadow twisted and coiled into a vast abyss. Traeth felt his very essence being sucked into that abyss. Never had he known such terror as he gazed into his own evil—the reflection of himself when there is no light. Fear overwhelmed him as he was engulfed by that darkness.

He shut his eyes, knowing that to look more would be to destroy his sight forever, for the mind could not comprehend the despair, the hopelessness and the lack of breath in that place.

He cried aloud in the Old Tongue; the words

exploded, shimmered and disappeared in a ghostwind of formlessness. He could recall neither his name nor his whereabouts.

And then he reopened his eyes. He had unmasked himself, and had discovered that what he most feared in himself was also what he most loved. With this newfound awareness, a pinpoint of light appeared in the void, and with all his being he sought it, longed, yearned, and reached for it . . . embraced it.

Memory returned.

He was Traeth of Rhune, Mage of the Dragon's Mouth, come in search of his beloved in the palace of the Sidhe.

He breathed deeply, and saw another face reflecting beside his own. The pure essence of beauty was embodied in Arrah's face, fine-boned, oval-eyed, her hair a sparkle of stardust. Her features were brushed with compassion and serenity shone in her wide, colorful orbs.

Those eyes met his own through the chill medium of the mirror. She said nothing.

He whirled around. "Milady, Arrah of Myr!"

His mouth agape, he looked at Ghillie in confusion.

He turned back to the mirror and saw himself no longer old, but youthful.

"Troth!" he gasped, as if it might be the very first gasp of an awakened soul.

With his fingertips, he traced the smooth skin of his face. Strength and vigor were flowing back into his body. He could see clearly and hear distinctly.

Again he looked to Arrah's reflection beside his own in the mirror. Again he turned away and saw only old Ghillie.

He moved to Ghillie, holding her quizzing gaze, and cupped his hands over her narrow, bent shoulders. How fragile she was, and how precious.

"Dear Ghillie, why didn't you tell me?" he asked

quietly. She answered him with silence, her eyes drenched with sadness, and ruefully he recalled all his coarse words and actions.

His hand slowly lifted, coming to her wrinkled chin, then tracing the rise of her cheek. "Oh, Ghillie, I would be old once more if regaining my youth means losing you. I would do anything."

She remained curiously still, staring at him. Then, a wry little smile curved her lips. "Kiss me," she whispered.

Softly he said, "Aye, love, I can do that."

He bent, bringing his mouth down on hers in a kiss.

The shift in his body came immediately.

He was old once more.

Traeth was gallant, but not so gallant as to hide his shock. "Sorcery be damned!" he cursed in her face.

Her rheumy eyes twinkled as she laughed quietly. "What did ye expect?"

He sputtered a moment, and then he too began to laugh, a deep-chested, full-out mirth that rang through the palace halls and corridors.

"'Tis a high price, but seems the only way ye have of paying for the unearned joy that loving me brings ye."

His arms tightened around her. "Oh, Ghillie or Arrah . . . whoever you are. I don't know whether to choke you or bless the fates for setting you in my path. I want to pull the soul out of your body and bring it together with my own in a place where there is no youth or old age."

"Och," she balked. "That might hurt!"

"Ghillie," he pushed on, "I'm wanting to be romantic with you."

"Then be so, milord! We've enough magic and illusion," she offered with scolding in her voice. "I'll have fewer words of romance and more kissing, please. Me lips may be a withered, thin line, but I'm not so shriveled that there isn't still heat in them.

Gather yer decrepit desire together and give me a kiss."

He did.

And what a kiss it was! The sun, moon and stars rise because of such kisses. In that moment both risked to love limitlessly—beyond youth, beyond old age—and the light of stars joined. Their hearts merged, healing, creating hope and unifying their old souls with the simple presence of love reborn.

In the midst of love's illumination, their bodies were liberated and the last guises of enchantment, along with the obstacles of fear, doubt and denial, dissolved.

They gazed at each other with beginners' eyes, free of illusion. All was new between them.

Like an ethereal icon, Arrah stood before Traeth, her senses swirling with anticipation. The chamber light lent a sharp outline to the otherworldly appearance of his now-youthful features. Yet, as clearly as she saw him, it was difficult for her to tell what he was thinking.

After a minute he reached out a careful hand to stroke a drift of hair from her forehead, cupped her fingers in his own and touched them to his lips.

"Milady." The single word was a caress. He folded her tenderly in his arms.

Arrah took her time before speaking, mainly because she didn't know what to say. Should she ask forgiveness for having deceived him in the guise of Ghillie? Nay, she thought, not unless he asked forgiveness for having locked her in the tower. Aye, that was all past and did not matter anymore.

He released his arms and, slipping a hand in hers, stepped back. "We've had quite the adventure. What do you wish to do now?"

The question off-balanced her. She touched her forefinger to her chin thoughtfully. "Mayhap you have asked me a question I cannot answer."

"Och! Ye don't think the earth and sky will fall upon me, do ye?" he mimicked in Ghillie's brogue.

"I would not be too shocked if they did; for a moment past, it seemed as if heaven moved above us."

Attractive creases softly bracketed his smile. "More the like we moved from earth to heaven."

Behind him the gossamer curtains waved floatingly and Arrah saw the glimmer of stars in the night sky above the garden. She held Traeth close and said, "You asked me what I wish now. I will be honest. We must leave tonight, as soon as possible. Modhan warned us not to sleep where we have drunk or eaten. Time is different between the two worlds. If we stay long we will begin to forget. I must have my swan skin, Traeth. You must return it to me, or our pure love will turn dark once more."

"How do you know this?"

"I know it. In my bones, I know it. If I do not have my swan skin I cannot return to Myr. Myr is my home, the heart of my wildish nature. Imagine yourself never seeing your loch again. That is how it would be for me not to return to Myr."

"Aye, I understand now," he confessed. "Before, I was driven by my own needs and desires. I thought that by taking your swan skin I could fly."

"You cannot use another's wings to fly. You must find your own."

"I know that now. You shall have your swan skin, milady. We will leave." He released her, then took up a brilliant golden cloak and put it over her shoulders. Bowing, he held the curtain aside for her.

His arm circled protectively around her shoulders, they moved forward. Arrah felt uplifted and clear-seeing as they walked through the courtyard.

The moon rose, a yawning grin in the sky, as Traeth led his black destrier from the palace stable. No one seemed to care or to even notice them now that they were not old.

Outside the palace gate, Arrah leaned into his warmth and moved with the horse's steady gait. "One night to the river," said Traeth.

"But how will we cross? 'Twill be many a day before a moonless night."

"Cross we must, or stay in Sidhe and remain forever young."

"Do you wish it?"

"'Tis tempting after being 'awld,' but I am a mortal man, Arrah. My life is in a mortal world. And what of you?"

"I am a wild thing. My life is in a wild world."

"Then we are yet companions of the road."

"For a time we are that," she agreed, turning her face up to his.

He kissed her, holding the moment as he would hold a treasure. She was a wild thing, and he knew she would leave him.

Chapter
12

On the return journey, as they entered the grove of hazel blossoms, Arrah touched Traeth's arm and asked him to stop.

"I want to drink from the spring once more," she announced with a toss of her golden head.

"You are braver than I," he said good-naturedly. He slipped down off the saddle and offered her his hand. "Now you have gazed into the mirror of unmasking, you've nothing to fear. Drink with me and we shall be refreshed. You've won the right to drink the spring's healing waters."

" 'Healing'?" he questioned, inclining his dark head toward the effervescing spring.

"Aye, healing. I know it did not seem so before, but 'twas all a gift, and being old before you were old was a healing of sorts."

He slanted a look at her and put his hand to her chin, stroking her bottom lip with his thumb. "I'm not so sure as you."

"Come, it will fortify us for the remainder of our journey." She took his hand and led him to the spring, where she filled the silver bowl and drank deeply of the sparkling water. It tasted even sweeter and more refreshing than before. Then she offered the bowl to him. "Drink."

He chuckled before he drank. "What a man will do for love is beyond imagining."

It was a new realm for Arrah, shimmering and golden; every physical sensation she had ever felt before became a pale cloud in comparison with this overwhelming sense of well-being. Traeth felt it also, she knew, for she saw the light of love in his eyes.

He leaned toward her. His lips touched her cheek, and she swayed under the power of his kiss. "Ah," she murmured, as pearls fell from her lips.

"Milady," he said with surprise, tiny diamonds falling from his own lips.

Arrah caught them in her hands, enthralled by their glitter. "You see, 'tis diamonds and pearls . . . diamonds and pearls between us."

Laughing, he asked, "How long is this to last that such treasures fall from our lips?"

"I should hope forever, my love, but I think only as long as we drink from the spring."

He caressed her shoulder, dropping his hand to her waist and pressing her close to him, the pearls and diamonds caught in the tangled strands of her hair. He put his arms around her, his palms flat on her back, and then his mouth came down upon hers; the kiss was a muffle of giggles as they exchanged diamonds and pearls in a sputter of mirth and pleasure.

"I fear we will choke on our good fortune," he said, lifting her upon the horse. She could only laugh as off they rode, leaving a fine trail of diamonds and pearls with their passing.

Their strong black steed galloped effortlessly across the flat expanse of the Plain of Wonder, a warm wind whipping at their backs. They reached the river the following evening. At the river's edge Traeth pulled up short, and stood in the saddle to stare across the breadth of the churning waters.

"What is it?" asked Arrah.

"A campfire."

"Redcaps?"

"Too tall," he replied, loosening the reins and pacing the horse up and down the riverbank.

Suddenly, he cried out, "'Tis the Fianna!"

"How would they be here?" she questioned.

He chuckled. "Mayhap your watching bird told them."

Again, he stood in the saddle, then hefted his sword and swung it whistling through the air, over the river and right into the midst of the Fianna camp.

A ballyhoo erupted among them, for they knew that sword. They rushed to the riverbank, waving arms, crying a raucous greeting.

His voice strong and clear, he chided, "Fine warriors you make! You wait until your enemies are on top of you before you see them."

A familiar figure moved to the forefront. Traeth recognized the heavy build of Dath Bright Spear in the flickering firelight. "My lord." His rumbling voice carried easily in the night air, despite the river's rushing.

"Speak freely, Bright Spear," encouraged Traeth. "We've too many years, too many battles, too much blood between us to remain estranged."

"I pledge my fealty to you, and my spear arm."

"I accept, and trust you've an idea in your head to get us across this river." He had ever counted upon Bright Spear to come forth in the dark hour with valor and ingenuity.

"I do, my lord. I shall throw my spear tied with a length of thick cord across to you and the Fianna in strength shall pull you through the current to safety."

"Come." Traeth dismounted, then helped Arrah off the horse.

"Can the Fianna match the power of the giant Modhan?" questioned Arrah, touching her feet to the ground.

"I do not know, but we must take that risk."

"And who's to risk first?" There was something of old Ghillie's audacity in her tone.

He chuckled. "The horse, my lady swan."

"Had your lady swan her swan skin, she might fly herself safely across."

"True, but she does not. She must shift about upon her own two feet—webbed though they be—like we mortal men."

"At least I am good at swimming," she said with bravado.

He smiled at her affectionately. "You are good at teasing as well."

On the opposite bank, Dath Bright Spear stood with his legs wide apart, testing and balancing the shaft of his spear in his hand. Then, with a shout, he ran forward and thrust the spear in a high arc into the air. The spear hummed and hissed like a living thing, its point tip landing so near Traeth that in the last second he had need to sidestep.

"Ho!" he called back. "Are you sure we've peace between us, Bright Spear?"

Bright Spear merely waved, then picked up the cord. The other Fianna stepped in line behind him.

Traeth secured the thick cord in two loops around the belly and neck of the horse and signaled the Fianna to pull.

Arrah watched anxiously, nibbling her lower lip as the horse whinnied, struggled and then disappeared into the swirling current. The Fianna began to chant in unison.

Straining, once Bright Spear came perilously close to the river's edge, but behind him the Fianna entrenched themselves and kept him ashore. When the horse emerged, hooves digging at the embankment, it was again white.

"Your turn, my lady swan," said Traeth, leaping to catch the shaft of the returning spear midair.

"You'll not tie the cord about my neck, will you?"

"Nay," he said, smiling suddenly, "though I won't deny there was a time that I wished to strangle the neck of 'awld' Ghillie."

"And what was that time?" she asked curiously.

"The time you thrust that iron poker at my throat."

"She did . . . not I."

"You did," he emphasized. "Don't deny it: You can be ruthless," he said, tightly securing the rope underneath her arms.

"No more than you," she defended. "You yanked your cloak from beneath an 'awld' woman and near rolled her into the hearth fire."

His rough tone softened. "We're quarreling, Arrah." He put his arms around her.

"Aye, we are that," she said in a small, halting voice. "I guess I'm afraid."

"I think we should cross together this time," he suddenly said. "If they can pull the horse to safety, surely they have the strength for we two."

"Aye," she agreed full-heartedly. "And if they don't, two lovers dying together makes better the romantic tale than one dying alone, don't you think?"

Looking straight into her violet eyes, he vowed, "We'll not die. We've been old together; now we must have a chance at being young together."

He tied the loop of cord around himself as well and wrapped Arrah in the safe cocoon of his embrace. Then he gave the go-ahead to Bright Spear. The Fianna gave a great shout and the cord went taut.

Fear coursed through Arrah as she fell into the cold, swirling waters. It was the same as before, the deep currents darkly grasping, except this time Traeth was there supporting her, keeping her face above the water so she might have blessed breath. It seemed an endlessly long time before she glimpsed the other bank and a big hand reaching out of the darkness. Traeth clasped the hand and lifted the two of them out of the river. Together they collapsed, their breath coming in gasps.

She sat up and curved herself back into the comfort of his strength. She was in his arms, warm and alive.

"Are you all right?" he asked tenderly, rising on bent knee.

"I will live." Her voice was shaky.

"Alas," he said softly, stroking the wet waves of her golden hair. "We've cheated death once more. The world must look elsewhere for a lovers' tale too tragic to be told."

"You know, my beloved," she whispered, not fully able to speak. "In our haste to cross you forgot to say where you had hidden my swan skin."

"That I did."

"It might be reassuring," she noted, "if you could tell me."

"It might be," he agreed.

But before he could speak, out of the shadows came a warrior, the firelight shining like blood on his gleaming armor.

"A horde of halflings is coming this way, upriver," he said, out of breath.

"My lord, do we fight or run?" came the questioning voice of Bright Spear.

Traeth was on his feet, lifting Arrah up alongside him. "We run first, and later, if need be, make battle." He turned to Arrah. "Are you recovered enough to ride?"

"Aye," she said, seeing a new facet of the man: the peaceful warrior.

"Then we shall leave. 'Tis not safe here, and our tale

may yet turn tragic." He ordered that the fire be doused and the hot ash thrown in the river, then they fled into the gathering night. Once they crested a rise and halted their mounts. In the distance near-total darkness reigned, save for the torches of the band of halflings.

"Remain here and see if they continue to follow us," Traeth asked the sharp-eyed Camlan the Unsmiling. He commanded the Fianna to pace their mounts by walking them as much as possible.

Camlan caught up to the rest of them at sunrise, just before they entered the woods of the Two Swallows. He declared that the halflings had veered east and seemed no longer a threat. Arrah, unaccustomed to riding, was reeling in the saddle, her face pale and weary.

Traeth looked down at her and said, " 'Tis not far to the loch. Can you ride more or do you wish to rest?"

"I can," she said doggedly.

"You are in a hurry to get back your swan skin," he said, attempting to banish his own dread that she would soon leave him. He was not savoring the emptiness of life without her—yet the panic he'd felt before was no longer there. The days of searching for her, yearning for her seemed a bad dream. He no longer wished to be enchanted. If parting from her was the price of a clear-eyed, free-spirited love, then he would pay that price.

The morning was bright and a fresh breeze rustled the treetops. When the Fianna emerged from the forest shadows and beheld the Loch of the Dragon's Mouth, Arrah's eyes widened with anticipation. Birds sang, animals scuttled through the undergrowth, an expectancy hung over the loch and hills like an impending birth. Promise flickered just on the edge of vision as the horses stepped boldly into the sunlight, manes tossing and tails swishing.

A sudden Arrah knew! She knew that it was time to awaken Sib from chrysalis. The life around the loch awaited her metamorphosis, for with it would come a new infusion of love's essence into the realm of men.

"I must go to the cave of the dragon's hoard," she said to Traeth.

"You know then," he replied.

"Know what?"

"That is where your swan skin is hidden."

"'Tis? But we looked there, Sib and I. We found nothing."

"I hid it beneath a stone slab, my love."

Arrah ruminated over this disclosure. Mayhap the hand of fate had stopped her from finding her swan skin. Even in the world of men, she realized, she had to trust that all good things come in all good time.

At that moment her attention shifted. Across the sky appeared, snowy and huge, five swans winging toward the loch. The swans circled above twice, thrice, coming lower each time. Then, with a flapping of wings, they skidded over the loch surface, their legs splaying the water into a series of silvery arcs. Alighting silently, they closed their wings.

"You must command your Fianna to keep their bows at their sides," she said, clutching Traeth's arm. "These are my kinswomen."

"Your kinswomen? Why have they come?" he asked, continuing to guide the party down a track to the mouth of the cave at lochside.

"'Tis the knowing that my sister Sib is to awaken from chrysalis."

"She is in the cave," he stated with understanding.

"Aye," she replied, waving her hand with greeting to the swans floating on the water. The swans moved to the water's edge and before all eyes shed their swan plumage and transformed into the fairest of women.

"Oh, Terwen, you've come," cried Arrah, slipping

from the saddle before Traeth could help her down. She ran to embrace Terwen and the others.

"Where is Sybil?" asked Terwen, standing regally in the long white shimmer of her swan cloak.

"Inside the cave. Come." Arrah took her hand and beckoned Traeth to follow.

Inside the cave the piles of gemstones and treasures shifted and sparkled in the light of the luminous orbs. Terwen turned her head and made comment when she heard the sweet strains of the Lyre of *Guivre*.

Arrah pointed to the chrysalis. "'Tis there."

The women stood in a half-circle around the chrysalis. They began singing, a singing that was rarely heard in the realm of men. It was hauntingly fey. It could soothe the rabid beast and calm the most violent warrior; it could lift the heaviest heart and break the hardest.

Arrah breathed into her palms before bringing her fingers together, and then she lowered her head and called upon her inner strength. Light radiated at the tips of her fingers. It faintly pulsed with her heartbeat. She put her hands on the chrysalis and began singing the song of awakening.

"Awaken the heart of freedom, deep within your soul. Flying high, circling the universe on wings of pure light. Born of water, born of earth, born of air. Let your sweet spirit arise, you who ever would be free."

She opened her eyes. The chrysalis was bright with a silver ghostfire, illuminating the slim silhouette of Sib inside.

Then the light was gone and the chrysalis slowly cracked open. Arrah felt so much excitement, it took all her effort to stand patiently by and allow Sib to rise and step out by her own power.

The others looked on, their faces filled with anticipation.

"Arrah!" cried Sib, opening eyes that swirled bright as fox fire. "Terwen . . ."

Sib had transformed. She was now a woman. Her hair was long and gold—a shade lighter than Arrah's. There were other changes also: her height, her face, her skin . . . Her chest was flat no longer, but had the curve of soft breasts; her voice rang with a deeper vibrancy.

"How do you feel?" Arrah asked.

"Different." Sib stepped out, tracing the curves and smooth flows of her body. For a long moment she examined the changes through tears of joy.

Arrah wept—for the Sib she now saw, and for the Sib who was lost forever. . . .

Sib sat beside the pool and leaned over to gaze into her own reflection. She splayed her hair through her fingertips, smiling, pursing her lips haughtily and finally sticking out her tongue with impish delight.

" 'Tis myself I still am, Arrah." She raised a slim, elegant hand in the direction of Traeth and said, "Do you recognize me, Mage of the Dragon's Mouth? Am I still wood rat ugly?"

Traeth bowed deeply. "Nay, milady. I was a fool in ever saying so. But beauty is deceptive, and I caution you not to let it go to your lovely head. I've learned my own hard lessons on that account." He looked over to Arrah, the corners of his mouth humbly downturned.

"Where is that Unsmiling Camlan?" asked Sib guardedly.

"Outside the cave," Traeth said. "Do you want me to call him in?"

"Nay, milord." She stood up. "I intend to recover my own swan skin and be off to Myr. I only asked to be sure of his whereabouts, for I do not wish to lose my swan skin to him as my sister Arrah did to you."

The women looked at Traeth. He felt the reproof in their gazes and knew it was time for the inevitable exchange to pass between Arrah and himself. He walked over near the pool, lifted the flat stone and retrieved Arrah's swan skin. As he ran his fingers over the soft feathers, its silken, sensuous touch sent ripples through him. He held it up.

She took a step closer. "My cloak."

"Aye, my lady swan, your freedom." He knew that once he gave her the cloak she would be gone, and he would not see her again.

"It is very beautiful, Arrah . . . as you are yourself." His voice was husky. He placed the swan skin upon her shoulders; it was the most difficult thing he'd ever had to do. His hands lingered.

"Let us fly," said Terwen, a bit impatiently.

Wordless, they all walked to the mouth of the cave.

Sib touched Arrah's arm and pointed to the tower of the dragon's fire. "My swan skin is secreted within the rafters of the turret."

Traeth shaded his eyes with his hand and stared across the loch to the tower. He turned to the waiting Fianna. "Camlan, you will carry the lady swan upon your horse to the castle. Upon your oath of honor as a Fiannan, assist her in retrieving her swan cloak, that she may fly free to her homeland."

Sib was obviously taken aback by this command. Arrah whispered, "Do you fear going with him?"

Covering her mouth with her hand, Sib whispered in return, "The fever of wanting him is past. I cannot believe that I ever cared a whit for him at all. He is vain as a peacock and treated me rudely. But I will go with him, for he is under oath. Look"—Camlan had dismounted and with his full attention awaited her— "he is the gallant now that I am beautiful. Men are beyond my understanding."

"Mine as well," returned Arrah softly, nudging Sib forward.

Camlan had removed his own cloak and now offered it to Sib, for she was wearing nothing. Innocently unconscious of the effect of her nudity upon the lusty eyes of the Fianna, she lifted her chin and looked down her nose at him. "See me, Camlan the Unsmiling, for 'twas not so long ago I was not fine enough to touch the hem of your cloak. Now, you offer it to me, but I shall scorn you as you once scorned me." With that, she climbed into the saddle by her own power.

Camlan stood stunned. His eyes widened and his mouth dropped open. "You . . . you can't be—"

"I am!" she said proudly.

He lowered his gaze as though in shame. There was a tension in the slightly averted profile as he remounted behind Sib. Fascinated, Arrah watched as the two rode off toward the castle. She wondered if Camlan would ever recover from the shock of Sib's transformation.

She felt Traeth's touch upon her elbow and turned to his voice. "My lady swan, will you walk with me beside the loch?"

"Aye," she acquiesced, and leaving the others she moved within the protective circle of Traeth's arm. The pair walked past the great boulders and down the twisting path to the water. For a long time there was silence between them. Arrah's emotions were in a churn over this bittersweet parting. Traeth stooped and picked up a flat stone, then tossed it and watched it skip lightly over the surface.

He finally spoke. "So," he began, "all in all, how have you liked your adventure in the world of men?"

She felt unable to find a way to express it, so she shrugged.

"You are at a loss for words?"

She nodded, but inside sadness welled like an overflowing spring. How she would miss him.

Laughter softened his dark eyes. She had forgotten how appealing and tender his face could become, how the corners of his dark eyes could relax into an endearing crinkle of smile lines.

"Kiss me," she asked thickly.

Caught by surprise, he lifted a dark brow. "You need never ask, my lady swan." He moved to her.

With softened eyes, they held each other's gaze until his hands came gently to rest on her shoulders and he bent forward to touch her lips. His mouth pressed against hers, drinking her sadness, feeding her his, breathing in the heat and wild scent of her body.

In a voice he could barely manage to keep under control, he said, "Arrah . . . sweet Arrah. I wonder what would happen if you stayed."

Suspended in tenderness, the impression of his mouth still upon hers, she opened her lashes, and her eyes met his with heartrending honesty. "I have stayed overlong already. When a swan maiden is gone too long from home, she loses herself. If we stay too long in the realm of men we lose our wildness and can no longer remember who or what we are about. Our eyes no longer sparkle, our bones grow weary and our skin dries out. Please understand that if I wait too long, I will forget the way back to Myr."

"Then you must leave, but ever know that I shall love you now and beyond death." He held her close, stroking her hair with his palm. "In between twilight and dawn, in between breath and sigh, if we never cross-path again, I will ever whisper your name, my lady swan."

From behind them came Terwen's voice. "'Tis time to fly, Arrah."

Arrah drew back. She saw a lone swan floating nearby on the loch and knew it to be Sib awaiting them. Terwen and the others were already walking down to the water and one by one transforming into swans.

Arrah looked at Traeth, his eyes heavy with unshed tears. Tears trembled in her own eyes. Without another word, she parted swiftly from him. Alongside the other swans she took to the air, her large wings ruffling the waters of the loch, while tendrils of sunlight flashed off her feathers. She circled once over the loch and the lonely figure left standing on the shore, then turned and set out for the east, and Myr.

Chapter

13

Time lost all meaning for Traeth; day drifted imperceptibly into night and back into day again. He measured his life in the waxing and waning of the moon and the appearance and disappearance of stars across the night sky. The fire of starlight matched the fire that still burned in his heart for his lady swan. Carne had told him that time would heal the relentless loneliness and emptiness that encased his heart, but he'd not found it so. True, he sometimes found peace in the knowing that somewhere in a land beyond Arrah gazed at the same starry heaven as he did; but in most moments that was meager consolation.

Ofttimes at dusk, he would row the curragh out to the middle of the loch, settle himself comfortably upon his back in the silence and count shooting stars through the night. His mother had once told him that each time a star fell a soul was borne to earth, but in his current state he believed that it was more the like a heart was broken. He had learned now that the gift of love was pain . . . pain and more pain. But he'd no wish to return to his old self—the self that did not love. The man who had armed his Fianna as well as his heart was gone. Knowing Arrah had changed his life; he couldn't go back even if he wanted to. But mayhap he had reached the limits of his ability to suffer.

Looking up at the vast stillness of stars, he cried aloud, "How many times must a heart break?" Mountain, loch and heaven surrounded him in a blanketing silence. A still presence within him listened, and what he suddenly heard was the simple beating of his own heart. And somehow that sacred rhythm was answer enough.

One night, as the moon reflected in a full, round blossom across the black waters, he stood by the loch where first he'd met Arrah and gazed into the ebony depths. A tiny splash disturbed the silence of the night. He looked up as a snow-white swan appeared from the rushes that bordered the loch. He dared not hope. Mayhap the appearance of this swan was nothing more than a sign, a sign telling him to carry on.

"Tirra lirra," came a greeting.

He straightened.

"I'm sorry. I did not mean to startle you."

The voice was soft and gentle, and familiar.

Before his eyes Arrah arose from the loch, her swan plumage falling magically from splayed fingertips.

He swallowed hard and blinked in an attempt to be sure she was no illusion.

"My beloved," she called, "you do not imagine me. I am real."

He only half-believed that she was there. She stood before him, her mosaic eyes alight with love. For a second his gaze studied her face, and then he reached out with one long, slender finger and touched the wisps of hair at the side of her head, tracing the outline of her cheek. Her long lashes lowered and she leaned into his caress.

"Why did you return?"

"I could not stay away. 'Twas the longest moon month of my life. I felt as if I carried another person within me—you. I had to come back. Terwen said that on the full moon I might pass between the two realms safely. I have come to sing my love lilt. I wish to bond with you my life long and beyond. Do you wish it as well?"

"'Tis my heart's desire—but you cannot stay in my world."

"True, but I can come and go freely, if you will but promise never to withhold my swan skin."

"I give you my oath as a warrior of the Fianna and as the Mage of the Dragon's Mouth," he pledged with fierce adamancy.

"An oath made can be an oath broken," she answered in a serious voice.

"Then you must trust," he said finally. "I give you my oath, my heart, and my love. . . . What more can I give?"

"Naught," she conceded.

He folded her tenderly into his arms and brought his lips down upon hers. She began to sway under the powerful feelings he evoked in her. In his arms she felt at home; not even the peace of Myr could match the joy of being in his embrace. Aye, she would trust him to death and beyond.

She remembered their first meeting by the loch—the aroma of the night, the sounds of the waves lapping along the shore. She remembered their thundering ride to adventure and the gift of the spring in Sidhe—diamonds and pearls sparkling like stars in the deep heaven. She remembered his lovemaking emblazoning her body like a dragon's fire. All this remembering had returned with a single kiss.

"Ah, love," she whispered. "I have found my home in a land of kisses and dragon's fire." And she knew that only love could heal the wound that love opened.

SWAN STAR

In that knowing she surrendered to him, and in surrendering, trusted.

He slipped his hands down until they were cupping her buttocks and lifted her to him with a firm pressure, and the cloth and cloak that separated skin from skin did not impede the tingling flow of desire between them.

In an ancient ritual of disclosure, she let her swan cloak slide off her shoulders. He drew back, removed his cloak and spread it upon the earth. He quickly undressed. Starlight lent sharp outline to his rugged face, his manly form and—although perhaps only Arrah could have seen it—his vulnerability.

Lithe, dangerous and ardent, he stood naked before her, then crossed the small space between them and pulled her close. She felt the heat of his skin against her own. His fingers dove into the soft tangle of her hair to bring her face close to his. His mouth hovered above hers, warming her lips, caressing them with his breath. Then her lips parted, permitting him access to the fleshy confines of her mouth, and her senses filled with the taste of him.

All time, realms and kith dissolved into spirit. They fell together like entangled thistle down caught in a passing whirlwind and collapsed breast to chest upon the cloak.

She began singing her love lilt, the song of bonding that was hers alone. "I am all things that begin in the earth, and within my womb dawn first opens. My waters pour through your parched spirit. Rest here in my heart."

She kissed his forehead and each eye in turn, saying, "Bless your sight to see your path and mine." Then, to his lips: "Bless your lips and mine that we may speak truth between us."

He received her ministering with love-light shining in his eyes and long-denied desire rioting in his veins.

209

"Oh, my lady swan—the long hours, days, nights, eternities without you," he said in a hoarse whisper.

The wind-dusted smell of her skin was so sweet to his senses that it made his head reel. The pink tip of her tongue tripped over his chin and descended in earthy, lacing patterns to the dark nipples of his furred chest.

"Bless your heart that it be open to me and mine to you," she continued, her tongue moving lower. "Bless your manhood, for all acts of love and pleasure." Her body pressed close to him, her breasts a soft, thrusting caress against his hips.

"Every part of you is blessed by me, every part of you is loved by me."

"Arrah," he moaned, "open your thighs to me—my need runs ahead of your blessings."

"I am dying for you, my love," she admitted with the insatiable hunger of longing.

"My lady swan, 'tis time to fly where stars are born."

With searing tenderness, he rolled her upon her back and looked into her moon-colored eyes, bright with the flame of passion's arousal. Gathering her into the curve of his own body, he eased himself into her melting warmth.

As he arched to the silken heat of his engorged manhood, her eyes widened. He gazed down through the many layers of iridescent sheen, and all his senses awakened to the exquisite wonder as on slow wing their spirit dance began.

He felt the softness of her breasts rise and fall in rhythmic coursing against his chest. He put his mouth on hers, suckling tenderly on her upper lip, using his tongue and lips to imbibe the moist underflesh. He felt her hands grasp the lean hardness of his buttocks, pressing him into her.

"Arrah . . . sweet Arrah!" he groaned, full-throated, as he thrust deep his shaft into the delicious darkness of her womb. His strokes became more powerful, like lightning and thunder over mountain peaks or gales lathering the seas.

Their hips undulated, falling, rising, merging into being, into nothingness—forever, incessant like the tides. Their union became a dazzling soul flight, a delirium of ecstasy.

The air rustled with the wind of wing and grace as Arrah transformed into swan, her feathers spreading toward heaven, where every unbound heart sings in flight. She soared on dream currents high above the earth, beyond the light of sun and moon . . . to star.

Around her the stars seemed to begin a slow whirl and to brighten and pulsate. She became lost in the pools of silence, silence that stretches and connects stars, silence that connects the spirits and hearts of lovers. And she knew that in that space, in all the myriads of sparkling diadems within her grasp, the light of two stars joined in a love that expanded boundlessly . . . and then, just as quickly, she fell past the reach of star and moon and reshaped as woman.

She felt Traeth's heart pounding next to her own, and she held him close with joy and awe. His long length over her, she opened her eyes and looked up, beyond Traeth's head to the heavens. A shooting star arced across the sky, and then another, like dragon's breath on a frosty night. Peace whirled through her as she met Traeth's gaze.

"Beway, my love," he said. "'Tis to heaven and back again we've gone."

"Aye, at long last I've touched a star."

"Mayhap," he chuckled disbelievingly.

"'Mayhap'?" she echoed with an impish smile. "The Mage of the Dragon's Mouth doubts me?"

She held out her hands, and upon her palms and slim fingers a silver shimmer of stardust glistened in the moonlight.

His eyes widened with wonder. "Oh, Arrah, I'm ever the fool to doubt you . . . a swan maiden."

"Musha, look at yer own hands," she said with the words and tone of Ghillie's mockery.

He turned his hands over, and there too was the glimmer of stardust. "Troth!" he exclaimed.

"Tirra lirra," said Arrah, the dazzling color of her cheeks framing a lopsided smile that was just sardonic enough to taunt him. " 'Tis clear ye accompanied me through the sky, me own true luv."

Irresistible laughter swallowed him. Wiping the teary mirth from his eyes, he returned in a hushed and heartfelt voice, "Aye, me lady swan, in 'awld' age and youth's beauty, ye are ever me own true luv." And then, he kissed her with never-ending simple tenderness.

Author's Note

I would like to credit research sources I have used in writing this story: *The Enchanted World Series*, published by Time-Life Books; and *Irish Folk and Fairy Tales Omnibus*, by Michael Scott. I also want to give credit to authors Marianne Williamson, Robert A. Masters and Clarissa Pinkola Estes for the mind-expanding influence of their writings upon my life.

Like most children, I loved fairy tales. Now, as a grown-up, I'm writing my own versions of some of my favorite tales—tales of the wild soul. I am a wild soul in a civilized world, and the swan maiden stories in some part symbolize my own quest to recapture my wild spirit.

I like to hear from my readers. Write:

Betina Lindsey
550 South 300 East
Centerville, Utah 84014

THE ENTRANCING NEW NOVEL FROM THE
NEW YORK TIMES BESTSELLING
AUTHOR OF *PERFECT*

Until You

by

Judith
McNaught

COMING SOON IN HARDCOVER FROM
POCKET BOOKS

POCKET
BOOKS

987-01

Printed in the United States
By Bookmasters